STEFAN

THE *Marquette* FAMILY BOOK THREE

NATIONAL BESTSELLING AUTHOR

TRESSIE LOCKWOOD

STEFAN

The Marquette Family

Book Three

CHAPTER ONE

The music blared in Talicia's ears and pulsed in her chest. She was used to it. In fact, she enjoyed it. Her nights wouldn't be complete if she couldn't come to the club. This was her place, her empire so to speak. No one could take it away from her.

Hiding a half grin, she moved about the crowd, nodding to those who acknowledged her and touching the backs of some. One of the regulars tried grabbing her hand to lead her onto the dance floor, but she resisted him, waggling a finger in his face. She didn't dance, not when she was working. Her gaze was always roving the crowd, looking for areas that could use improvement, customers that could use prodding to enjoy themselves more.

Of course, it went without saying she watched for fools who thought they could disrupt the well-oiled machine that was her club. They ended up on the street—on their asses if necessary—and Talicia didn't need to rely on the bouncers she employed to get it done either. There was nothing she liked more than to surprise a hulking jackass with how strong she was at her size.

"Licia." Her twin brother wrapped an arm about her shoulders and leaned his cheek against hers. She rolled her eyes and patted his head. "Get off. I have to focus."

"Girl, you know you got this. Our club is on fire tonight, and nobody's going to mess it up."

"It's on fire because I stoke it and make sure it doesn't get out of hand."

"Come have a drink with me."

She managed to get out of his hold without knocking his scrawny tail on the floor, but he wouldn't back off. Tyjon pulled her in the direction of the bar and held up two fingers to one of the bartenders.

"Ty, I'm not drinking tonight."

"Yes, you are." He shoved a glass full of pale liquid into her hand and knocked back one of his own. She gave in because it was easier to deal with him that way. He grinned and wiggled a hand, indicating her entire body. "See? The bitch aura is easing already."

She pursed her lips. "No, you didn't just call me a bitch, Ty."

He fluttered heavily made up eyelashes at her. "I said *aura* de bitch."

She held up a finger in his face. "You're not funny."

"I'm fierce though, right?" He did a twirl. "Look at how I'm working this outfit, Licia. You can't tell me I don't have all eyes on me tonight."

Talicia laughed and shook her head. Okay, she had to admit Tyjon looked good in anything. He always did command a room, so confident in his sexuality and so full of personality. She adored her brother, and she would do anything for him. In fact, her life had been devoted to making sure he was okay.

"Every eye is on you because you're loud and bright," she teased.

He pouted, and she kissed his cheek.

"Aw, I'm just playing. You look great."

His smile lit up the room. "Thanks, 'lil sis. So is he coming tonight?"

She ran a hand over the back of her head, smoothing her hair. "I'm ten minutes older than you."

"But is he coming?"

Talicia swirled to face the stage. The live band played, one night on a limited schedule. She knew what Tyjon was asking, but to answer meant stirring up a conversation she didn't want to have. Instead, she leaned an elbow on the bar and accepted a second glass. This one she sipped. Tyjon knew she didn't drink much. Yet, he was right. Sometimes, she felt like she needed it. Nights like tonight.

"Yeah," she said at last. "He's supposed to be coming."

Whenever the band was playing was a night he might call her to tell her he would be there. So many times, the call didn't come, and the only person she admitted her bitter disappointment to was herself. Not even to Tyjon, but he knew.

"Licia, he—"

"Don't start, Ty."

He pursed his lips. "It's because I love you that I say anything. Has he ever once offered to introduce you to his family, or for that matter to let them know you exist?"

"Let it go," she bit out and stirred to traverse the room. He followed. When they were near her office, he grabbed her arm, and she paused, sighing. "I don't want him to introduce me. We both agreed."

"Yeah, but he should have insisted. He should have been proud to show you off. Maybe he thinks you're not pretty enough or that…"

He went on, but Talicia had stopped listening. Her brother meant well, but he had hurt feelings—again. She didn't wear them on her sleeve for anyone to know. As far as Tyjon or the friends and acquaintances in her life knew, Talicia was hard as nails. Tyjon had hinted that she was a bitch, and she supposed she acted that way a lot. She didn't care if they thought of her that way because she used it to survive. The world they lived in almost required it. On the other hand, having Tyjon say she wasn't considered to be pretty enough, well, that scalded.

Talicia punched in the code to let herself through to the office. When her brother tried to follow, she shook her head and gave him the look that meant give her space or suffer the consequences. He backed off. She watched as he found a dance partner, a man he'd been teasing for a while now.

Talicia headed upstairs to her office and shut a second door there. The noise level from the music died down, and she dropped into a chair and shut her eyes. When she did, an image of a man with dark hair and frosted blond tips slipped into her head. The green eyes so full of gentle humor and all around happiness with life were what made her heart beat faster and stole her reason. Tyjon didn't know the truth. No one did. Not the full extent of her connection to her lover.

The panel to her right buzzed, and she stirred from her position to stab a button. "Yeah?"

Right away music interrupted her solitude, and a tinny voice informed her, "Your singer's here, Licia."

She stood and leaned over the panel to scan the crowd below. The two-way mirror kept anyone from seeing into her private booth, but she could observe them without issue. He stood at the foot of the stage, talking to one of the drummers and smiling.

Already Talicia's heart rate had kicked up, and she found it harder to draw in a breath. Recalling her brother's innocent comment from earlier, she glanced down at herself. Tonight she wore simple black slacks and a crisp white shirt. As she ran her hands over her chest, her palms barely registered the small rise in her breasts. She wished she had chosen something else. Anything would be more flattering to her figure—what little figure she had.

As Talicia descended the stairs to the main club area, she wondered what ran through his mind when he looked at her on any given night. Did he feel regret about the circumstances of their meeting? He had to be attracted to her on some level. After all, he kept coming to her bed. Not regularly though. Maybe they were coming to an end. She couldn't say she hadn't expected it long before now.

Music from the keyboard filled the air, and a new beat replaced what they pumped through the speakers. Talicia stumbled to a stop to watch him. He was born for the stage. He played it up, drawing in every person, male and female, to his performance. No one could ignore him.

Then there was the voice—that smooth deep voice that sang of love and heartache, longing, lovemaking in the wee hours. Talicia scanned the audience, and several women were casting out lures. Some were subtle, but one woman boldly weaved through the crowd and threw a slip of paper on the stage. She mouthed the words "call me," and he winked at her. Talicia rolled her eyes.

She moved farther along the crowd and spotted another familiar face, also casing the crowd. They were careful about those who entered the club. No weapons, but one couldn't be too careful. Her bouncers were trained. She trusted them, but Jerome was far more than a simple bouncer.

"Hey, Jerome," she said when they passed.

"Ms. Talicia."

She read his lips more than heard his voice. He was as big as a refrigerator. Despite his size he could move like an Olympic runner. She had seen him in action. He knew his stuff, and he would die for his employer. Period.

Talicia found a spot near a table and paused to watch *him* again. She couldn't help herself. His presence was so big he drew her attention just as he did that first night when he wandered into her club, a white man who looked like he was upper crust, slumming on her side of town. Well, they weren't the slums exactly, but still, the few white people who visited the club were lower to middle class. He had given off a scent of money from day one. Talicia hadn't known who he was, but Tyjon did, whose face was glued to the tabloid news when he wasn't in the club—both online and on TV.

"Damn, he looks so good I could eat him," a Latino woman said, who sipped a drink next to Talicia. She flipped long auburn dyed hair and licked her lips. Talicia realized it was the same woman who had approached the stage and tossed her number up there. She had a lot of confidence. "*Chico,* do you know if he's got a girl?"

Talicia bit down on her cheek. "Why don't you ask him?"

The woman's eyes widened, and she let her rude gaze rake over Talicia's slender figure. She'd had the same treatment a hundred other times and was used to it—not really. "Oh, sorry. You're a woman!"

Of course, everyone speaking in the club had to yell, but why did it seem a lull had risen in the noise to cause her shout to be heard more distinctly? Several heads turned in their direction. Talicia pretended an interest in something across the room while her anger simmered.

She counted and concentrated on breathing. The fact that she wasn't the most feminine looking woman in the world wasn't her fault. There was no reason to rearrange this woman's beautiful face. And she was beautiful, too, with luxurious hair, pouting lips, big boobs, and a figure any man would beg to touch.

"Well, it doesn't matter," she went on, dismissing Talicia as any type of competition. "I made sure he saw where I put my number. Those other bitches are copycats. He's going to come to me."

Talicia shrugged. She tried to school her expression to show she had no opinion on the matter. However, a stubborn desire to prove the woman wrong made her stay nearby throughout the performance. When the show came to a close, the deep sexy voice promised he would come again, and the women cheered.

He moved away from the keyboard and cupped his eyes against the lights. His gaze flicked over the crowd, and honestly Talicia couldn't tell if it lingered on her or on the Latino woman. Bouncers along with Jerome kept the other women at bay. He made his way through the crowd, and Talicia stared, taking in his broad shoulders and chest straining against his shirt. The tanned skin on his bare forearms reminded her of how he looked naked—perfection. She'd never been into white guys, but from the moment she met him there had been attraction between them.

"Told you so," the Latino woman said as she primped and straightened. She stepped into the aisle, blocking Talicia's view. He reached her and then stepped to the side to get around her.

"Excuse me," he muttered in his deep tone. He reached Talicia and caressed the skin on the inside of her wrists. "Licia."

She coughed and cleared her throat. Emotion overwhelmed her until she got a grip on herself. "Stefan."

Her heart thundered. She couldn't say anything else.

"Can you get off right now?"

"I'm afraid I've got a couple more hours to go."

"Then I'll wait for you."

Why oh why did he have to say it like that? She waved a hand and tried for a do whatever you want attitude, but he strummed her other palm with his fingertips. Damn if she didn't tremble a little. Only Stefan could make her defenses crumble with a touch that gentle.

"Okay." She didn't think he heard because the music had come back on. Talicia eased around him, and she met the angry gaze of the woman. "What were you saying?"

A string of curses in Spanish flew from the woman's mouth, but Talicia ignored her and kept moving. The rest of the night, she worked to keep her head on the job, avoiding eye contact with Stefan. Women approached him. He entertained them chatting and dancing a little, nothing too close or too intimate. She had learned early on he had a way of seeming available and flirting without actually doing it. Talicia had told him it didn't matter to her one way or another, which wasn't true, but the man had this weird honor system. He wasn't her first man, and she had never trusted anyone, so Stefan's attitude had taken her by surprise.

At last, the time rolled around to close. Talicia covered her mouth, yawning. "Hey, let's clear it. I'm tired."

One of the bouncers smirked. "You mean you want to get to your toy."

She pinned him with a glare. "Whether I do or don't is my business, isn't it? Mind yours before I make you."

"Damn, Licia, ease up. I was kidding."

She said nothing, just looked at him. He stumbled over an apology. Within minutes the club was empty, and the cleanup began. She didn't need to stick around for that part, thank goodness. A squeal behind her brought her around. Tyjon skipped across the floor and launched himself at Stefan's back, grinning.

"Hey, baby, it's been what…a month? You never come around anymore."

Talicia shook her head. Her brother kept telling her Stefan was using her, but then whenever Stefan came around, he acted like they were old friends. Sometimes she thought he did it to see if it would make Stefan uncomfortable, but that wasn't Stefan's way.

Stefan grinned and accepted the hug. "Ty, how are you? Things have been kind of busy. It's not as easy to get away. Trust me, there's nothing I like more than to come here."

"Because we let you play the hot stuff, not just the elevator music in your restaurant."

Stefan laughed. "That and…" He let his words trail off, but his gaze slid to her. If she weren't so brown, she'd have blushed red.

Stuffing her feelings deeper, she approached them. "Come on. We can get out of here now. Ty, you coming, or you have a date?"

Her brother straightened and released Stefan. "I'm coming. Too tired, and turns out that bastard has a boyfriend. I don't play the other man role."

"Want me to show him something for you?"

A devious grin appeared on Tyjon's face. "No, I have my own plan for showing him."

"You kind of led him on a long time, didn't you, Tyjon?" Stefan said.

"That's different."

Stefan waited for Tyjon to explain, but she knew her brother. Talicia grabbed his arm, and they headed out of the club. "My car or yours?"

"Mine."

Talicia settled in the back seat next to Stefan. Tyjon rode in the front next to Jerome. "Do you ever drive yourself anywhere?"

He laced his fingers with hers in the darkness of the back seat, but they sat apart. Not even their shoulders touched. Tears pricked her lashes. He was ashamed, but so was she. She never pushed. What was wrong with them—with her? Tonight, she should let him go and tell him not to come back to her or the club.

"I would drive myself here," he said, "but I've never been successful at slipping away from Jerome. Also, some of the things that have happened, I don't want to leave him behind."

She tensed. "What happened? Ty didn't mention seeing anything in the news."

"Everything my family deals with doesn't make it to the media."

She studied his face. He appeared calm. "You never talk about your family."

Green eyes met her gaze and captured her heart as they always did. "You don't talk about yours."

Talicia gestured to Tyjon. "You're looking at it."

"Parents?"

"What about you?"

He grinned. "Fine."

What did that mean? He said no more, and she didn't push. They arrived at the apartment she shared with Tyjon and walked inside. Tyjon went to his room. Jerome settled himself in the third bedroom, which she had set up as a home office, and she and Stefan headed to her bedroom.

Stefan shut the door behind them, and before the latch caught he encircled her waist and drew her close to kiss her lips with hungry abandon. "Your mouth," he whispered when he raised his head, "is what I miss the most when I'm away."

"Stefan."

"Shh, kiss me again, my beautiful little wife."

CHAPTER TWO

A knife shot through Talicia's heart at his words. His wife. What he said was true. They were married, husband and wife, and they had been for eight months. Not once had they ever lived together. No one knew, including Tyjon. Her brother knew they were lovers, and so did the bodyguard. His family had no idea she existed.

Talicia kissed Stefan once and managed to wiggle free from his hold to put space between them. He moved toward the bed and began unbuttoning his shirt. Her pulse raced seeing the smooth taut skin coming into view.

Gasping for a breath, she half spun away. "About that, us being married. It was crazy. We didn't know what we were doing."

"We weren't drunk," he said.

She frowned at him. "No, we weren't, but we had just met the night before at the club."

"And made love all night."

"Yes," she croaked. "From what I've seen of you, it's just like you to be impulsive, do whatever pops into your head. I'm not like that. I have to make sure—"

"Make sure of what?" He strode over and grasped her

hand to tug her to him. Talicia tumbled against his chest and found she wanted to stay there forever. She shut her eyes as her fingers with a will of their own began exploring his body. The buttons on his shirt were a barrier, so she leaned back to finish undoing them. Stefan's warm skin drew her lips. She rained soft kisses on his chest, and he moaned.

If she could just turn down the attraction for a minute, she could think clearly when it came to him. Maybe that was the problem. This was a lust problem, and the long periods between seeing him made it harder to move on. If she got his cooperation, everything would be fine.

Talicia moved out of his embrace, but he caught her and drew her back. His big arms came around her from behind, and he held her in place with a gentle but firm hold. She wiggled just enough to feel his solid erection against her ass. She bit her lip.

"Let me go a minute, Stefan."

Right away, she found herself freed, and she could have wept. Talicia willed herself to move away from him and kicked off her shoes.

"You've cut your hair," he said.

She started. A hand went up to her head, and she smoothed the hair that was gelled close. Anger, sadness, and a slew of other emotions had hit her the other day, and she had whacked off most of her hair. Now it wasn't more than an inch long. She and Tyjon must look like identical twins.

"Yeah, I did. You don't have to like it," she snapped.

His eyebrows went up at her meanness. She regretted it. Most of the time she kept the attitude bottled when it came to him, but it wasn't easy. Not that she pretended, but Stefan didn't deserve a bitch for his lover.

Well, he's got one, so that's a moot point.

"You would be beautiful even if you were bald."

She rolled her eyes. "Whatever. I mean thanks, I guess."

"Talicia, come here, please." He held out his hand. She swayed in his direction but locked her heels to the floor. *"Please."*

"Stefan, we need to talk."

"We can talk after we make love. I've been dreaming about your body, and I can't wait to get you under me."

She panted. Taking in Stefan's size as he said stuff like that was killing her. Six foot two, built like a truck, and gentle as a lamb, he made her feel tiny under him. Most men did because she had a slender build, but with the others, she had to prove her strength. With Stefan, from the first night he produced a different emotion in her. One of being protected. The feeling was so at odds that when he flashed that ridiculously bright smile at her the next morning and said, "Let's get married, see what it's like," she had agreed on the spot.

She needed to be firm with him. "If we talk after we have sex—"

"Make love."

"—then we'll do it the rest of the night like usual. You'll get called home or to your restaurant or whatever. Or I'll have to get to the club to stop my fool partner from doing something dumb. Then I won't get to see you for…"

She trailed off because she heard the ache in her tone at the end. No matter what, she didn't want him to know how much she loved him. Damn, it was love after all. Whenever he left, the thought of not having sex didn't enter her mind but that face, that voice, his gentle embrace and kindness did.

Let it go, Talicia!

"I'm sorry, honey," he said.

"Don't call me honey," she groused. That hurt too much. "Listen, we made a mistake."

"It wasn't a mistake."

She blinked at him. Could he care about her the way she loved him?

"Nothing in life is a mistake, even if everything goes wrong. It's a learning experience. It's living, and I never apologize for it."

Her hopes fell. "Okay, then. Now it's better if we both experience divorce."

"Is that what you want?"

"We've been married almost a year, and we've never lived together. We haven't truly experienced marriage. We have a piece of paper. That's all. So, let's stop pretending and just dissolve it. What is it called? I think annulment?"

"We've been lovers all throughout. Annulment isn't possible."

"Then divorce."

His eyes went dull. The light almost never disappeared in his gaze, and it about killed her to see it now, especially since she didn't understand why. All she knew was she was causing it, and she wanted to put it back. Her response to Stefan was the same way she worked to make sure Tyjon was happy and had everything he needed.

"Stefan, I don't understand why you're hesitating." She moved up to him as he turned his back. He had slipped his shirt off, and she couldn't help exploring the tight muscles. His male scent, a mixture of sandalwood and soap, tantalized her nose. Their conversation was serious, but she had to press close and breathe him in. The crown of her head didn't reach the top of his shoulders. "We have to."

He rotated his shoulders, and she sensed an increase in his tension. "The only thing we have to do, Licia, is find our happiness. Currently, we're happy with being lovers."

She sighed and straightened. "What if I'm not happy?"

He whirled to face her and touched her waist. Her body lit on fire. "You're not? I don't please you? Tell me what you want, and I'll work harder to satisfy you. Or is it…"

An odd expression came over his face. She frowned. "What?"

"Is there another man you prefer? Someone you want to be with instead?"

She couldn't let him believe that ridiculous lie. Another man who could make her body feel the way he did? Who went to such lengths to make her come and looked the way he did? Hell no. She was twenty-nine and had a handful of lovers over the years. Every one of them insulted her figure straight out or they hinted around that they wished she had more meat on her bones and her breasts were bigger. One asshole, whose tooth she had knocked out with a punch to his jaw, had said she looked like a boy, and it grossed him out to have sex with her. Why the hell did he sleep with her then?

Thinking about the past brought a fresh bout of shame and hurt, and she spun away from Stefan before he could see it. Maybe this was why she had clung to him and said yes to his proposal—because she didn't think anyone else would want her.

I'm a woman like any other one. I deserve a man who loves me just like I am.

She spoke the words in her head, but she already

knew they were hard to believe and accept. Talicia hugged herself, and Stefan's arms came around her to cover her own. His hard body met hers, and she sank into his embrace.

"There's no other man," she said.

He kissed along the side of her throat, and she turned her head to invite one on the lips. Stefan's tongue slid into her mouth, and she moaned. He captured her chin to raise it higher and took the kiss deeper. Every nerve ending tingled, and her pussy clenched. He brought one big hand around to flatten on her belly and slid it lower. She didn't mean to give in, but she spread her thighs a little to let him cup her heat.

Stefan took his time raising his head, and he stared into her gaze. "The attraction between us is still too hot to let go. I thought it would burn down, and then we could walk away. Every time I touch you, I have to have you. I have to make you come, and I have to come inside you."

"Stefan," she whimpered. "Don't say that."

"It's true, isn't it?"

Of course it was true, damn it. "It's true that you're insane. I mean you're a billionaire, Stefan. Do you know what you're risking being married to me, having sex with me without a condom, and all the risks you're taking? You're too trusting."

"Do you want my money?"

She frowned and broke away from his hold again to face him. "Excuse me?"

He held up his hands. "To divorce me means you get a portion of my money."

"I—" She was too pissed to speak.

"You could also demand I take you to my house so you can move in and live as my wife in the open."

She stiffened. "You're not saying you want that."

"No, I'm not."

A knife stabbed her heart. "I don't want it either. I'm not living in your world. I have my own reasons for never wanting anyone to know about us being married."

"That's why I can come in you."

"Stefan! It could be a plot."

"Sure. I'll take the risk."

"You take too many risks."

He grinned. "What would life be without risks, and I'm not so protective over my money that I care about a wife taking half of it. It's just money. Someone else manages the boring parts. I was once poor, and I can be again. I don't care. All I care about is enjoying every breath I'm given. Life is a gift, and it's short. It should be spent doing the things I love, not worrying about who's going to fleece me."

"You seriously irritate me."

He grinned. "You turn me on."

"You're impossible to deal with." She paced. "So what you're saying is you want things to continue as they are? We stay married and continue as sometime lovers?"

"Yes, as long as we please each other."

"But when we don't and one or the other isn't satisfied anymore? What about then?"

"Then we deal with it at that time."

"Divorce?"

"Licia." His voice took on a firm tone she rarely heard from him. "Let's not mention that term anymore. You want me. I hear your body crying out for me, and mine is vibrating it aches for yours so bad. That's all that matters. I'm living for right now, tonight. I'm living to be inside you and nowhere else."

She shook from head to toe. Leave it to Stefan to

make sex sound like love. He had to know his words produced that effect. There was no way he didn't see it. No, of course he saw it. He knew she wanted him and would kill a bastard to get to Stefan. She just hoped he put her emotions down to physical and not those of the heart.

"Can I have you?" he asked gently, holding out his hand. "My wife. Can I lie between your legs and take you until neither of us can move?"

She stopped pacing. There wasn't a chance in hell she would turn him down.

CHAPTER THREE

Talicia moved to her closet and began unbuttoning her blouse. She kept her back to Stefan as she shed her clothes and soon stood in just her panties with no bra. A glance down reminded her of the smallness of her breasts and the narrowness of her hips. She looked like she didn't have a waistline.

The tiniest of curves along her middle and over her ass gave her a feminine appearance. She had spent a lot of time in a local gym training in self-defense, but she had learned to throw a solid punch in school.

Stefan's fingers wrapped around her upper arms, covering the defined muscle there. He drew her toward him, and her ass brushed his thigh. His cock had gone hard, and she felt it against her back. Stefan had never said she turned him off or reminded him of a man. He looked at her with such desire from day one, she responded to it and couldn't help herself.

"Licia," he whispered, his lips at her nape, "why do you turn away from me when you take your clothes off? I want to see you."

"You see me when we're in bed."

"I can't wait." He spun her around and tipped her chin up. "What's wrong? Didn't we settle things earlier?"

"You're such a man."

He gazed at his cock, straining toward her through the gap where he had opened his pants but hadn't removed them yet. "Last time I checked."

Talicia slipped around him, but she let his shaft brush against her side as she moved. "There were a lot of beautiful women in the club tonight. You could have had your pick of any of them. Every woman loves a musician."

"Is that what you're worried about? Me cheating?"

She ground her teeth with regret. Never let a man think she was jealous or hurt over him. That was her motto, and she had stuck to it from as far back as high school. Her response to their stupidity had always been anger. Now here she was whimpering about Stefan and those women. This was what she got for falling in love.

"No, I don't care what you do. You're a free agent."

He tugged her around at the edge of the bed and then lifted her onto it. She thought he'd toss her, but he placed her gently down and followed with his massive body. Her heart thundered at his delicious size and weight coming down on her. He tapped his knee against hers, and she spread her legs. Then he settled half on top of her and a good portion of his weight on the mattress.

"I'm not a free agent. I'm your husband."

"It's just an arrangement. Like I said, a piece of paper."

"A serious piece of paper."

She looked away. "Stefan, I'm not expecting anything from you."

He leaned down and teased her lips for a kiss. She gave into him and then winced when his belt buckle rubbed a bit too hard against her belly. He sprung away like he'd been stung. "I'm sorry. Are you okay?"

Talicia shoved his hands off her stomach. "I'm fine. The buckle scraped a little."

"Did it cut your skin?" He tried to look, but she smacked his hand.

"Just take it off."

He stripped in seconds. Her mouth watered as she took him in, loving every sinew and plane. She had never asked him, but she assumed Stefan worked out. The tone of his body seemed so incongruent with his personality, but she liked it. Just as that woman had said earlier, she could eat him up. In fact, she'd done so plenty of times. Talicia agreed with Stefan that their attraction hadn't lessened. If anything it burned hotter. Every time she saw him all she could think about was getting her hands on him. When he wasn't in her bed, her body went unsatisfied.

The mattress sagged under Stefan's weight, and Talicia rolled to face him. She brought her hands up to rest on his chest and nuzzled her lips against the base of his throat. He ran a hand along her arm and stopped at her elbow.

"Kiss me, Licia. I can't get enough of your mouth."

She raised her head and parted her lips. Stefan claimed them and stuck his tongue into her mouth. They moaned together as their tongues intertwined. A good ten minutes passed before he leaned back, and she struggled to catch her breath.

"In answer to your comment, there were a lot of women there. They don't matter. I like putting smiles on people's faces, male or female. It makes it more fun to know they're having a good time. At the end of the night, I know where I want to be, and that's here."

He punctuated his words by raising one of her legs and thrusting forward. The tip of his cock sliced between her folds and eased inside. She was already wet and ready for him. Stefan knew her body like no man before him. His thick cock sank deeper, and a tremor shook her to her core.

She clung to his arms, whining in pleasure. Stefan's dick was huge, and the first time he took her she thought he would kill her. She loved it because he stretched her walls and gave her such pleasure despite the pain.

Stefan had been funny too. He'd fallen on the floor, scared out of his mind. "I'm sorry, I'm sorry, I'm sorry," he'd chanted, face red hot. "You're so tiny. I hurt you. I never meant to. Please, forgive me."

Talicia had sat up, staring at this white man that was so worried about how she felt. She'd grown hotter for him, aching to get him inside her pussy. "It's okay. Come here. I want it."

"No." He looked so cute and embarrassed, trying to cover that massive tool he had lying between his legs. At first she began to think it was a ploy because he was turned off. Then she saw how it seemed to throb and was so tight. Stefan was sorry for hurting her, but as she leaned toward him he was looking from her breasts to her pussy and trying his best to calm down. "Maybe you should get dressed. We'll um…"

"You're not leaving this room before I come." She had lain on her back and spread her legs. Running a finger over her clit, she'd played with herself and squirmed while moaning.

The big man had sprung up from the floor and landed above her, staring. "That's not fair, Licia."

"I want to come." She pushed her fingers into her heat and pulled them out wet. He'd lost it then and had to finish what he'd started.

Tonight, when Stefan entered her, there was nothing but pleasure for both of them. He raised her legs high and climbed atop her. She knew being on top of her was his favorite position, but she liked to ride him just as much. Stefan was always gentle, but sometimes she liked it a tad bit rougher. She got that wildness when she took control. He was sweet enough to let her.

Stefan hiked her legs high enough that her ass rose off the bed. He leaned back so he could watch as his cock glided into her pussy and slid out. She whimpered his name and moaned, wiggling and arching to get all of him. Their bodies met and drew apart again. Even as Talicia's orgasm began to build, she wanted a steeper incline that meant a harder crash.

"I want to get up," she panted.

His eyes were shut, but he forced them open so he could keep staring at her naked body. "Not yet, honey."

He pumped faster. She scratched at the sheets and shook her ass as much as she could. Air hissed between his teeth. Talicia pushed at his chest. "Stefan."

He gave in and pulled his cock out of her. They switched positions, and she climbed atop him. He was so much bigger than her that her knees didn't touch the mattress when she straddled his waist. She braced herself on his chest, arched, and brought her pussy down on the head of his cock. He sank to the hilt, and she cried out in pleasure.

"Easy, my love," he whispered, but Talicia refused to take it slow. When she was on top, she ran things. Stefan could hold on for the ride.

Talicia leaned as far forward as she dared and braced herself on his chest. Then she came down fast on his cock, driving it deep into her pussy. Stefan's fingers squeezed her hips to keep control of how far he sank. No matter how much she tried to make him pound her, he wouldn't allow her to hurt herself. Still, she moved like lightning on his shaft, riding fast and grinding hard. Her orgasm skyrocketed, and her core muscles contracted until she had to clench her jaw not to scream her head off.

While they pumped together and she bounced, she rubbed her clit with her middle and ring finger, massaging it in a circle until she came again. Stefan called out her name, and she felt his hot seed burn up her insides. He went still, but she didn't climb off him.

"There's nothing's like coming in you," he said, watching her.

She melted. "I know."

All doubts about her body fell away right after she came and he released in her. She didn't know why it happened that way, but she always basked in it. While he stared at her, she played with her nipples and pinched them. He tried not to blink as she skimmed fingers down her belly to her bud. Stefan moved to an elbow to watch.

"Are you going to make yourself come again?"

"Do you want me to?"

"I love it when you come. Your expression is unbelievable."

She smirked. "You like watching me."

"Yes, do it for me, Licia." He stroked her inner thigh. "Come on me."

Inside her, his cock pulsed, and she believed she could feel it starting to swell already. He never stayed down long. His appetite for sex was huge, and it matched her own. That's why when he showed up they spent an entire night in bed. No sleep, just sex.

"I don't know if I can so soon. I've come twice

already. That second one is always the easiest."

"This isn't work. It's pleasure and fun. I know what you need."

He grasped her around the waist and raised her off his cock. She groaned at losing it, but he laid her on her back and followed her down. "No, Stefan. You already came in me."

"Yes," he insisted. "I'm going to lick you right here until you come. Then I'll do it again." He tapped her clit, sending zings all over her body.

"R-r-right there?" she stuttered.

He licked it. "Yes, right here."

Another lick, and she was gone. Just when she was at the edge of an orgasm, he crushed her into the bed and brought his big body down on top of her. His thick cock invaded her body, and he pumped into her. Both of them forgot themselves and the fact that they weren't alone in the apartment. Talicia shouted his name, and Stefan encouraged her to come. The dizzying ecstasy lasted the rest of the night, and they didn't stop until the sun rose over the horizon.

* * * *

Talicia left the room and Stefan sleeping in her bed to look in on Jerome. She'd forgotten to give him sheets and a spot to crash, but it looked like he knew the routine. He'd found the sheets and stretched his huge form over the couch in the third bedroom. She winced. At least the man should have pulled out the bed. He must have been uncomfortable all night.

In the kitchen, Tyjon played music and danced while frying bacon. Talicia rubbed at her temples. "It's too early for that noise, Ty."

He pursed his lips and tightened the belt on his lilac robe. "Excuse me, Miss Thing, but it is eleven o'clock, and I'm not the one that can't handle my liquor."

"No, but you're the one that pushed me to drink. My head hurts."

"It wouldn't feel so bad if you'd gotten sleep instead of screaming down the walls having sex."

Her teeth clacked together in her embarrassment. "Sorry. I didn't mean to be so loud."

Her brother grinned. "Makes me jealous. Let me try him out."

She snorted. "If you can seduce him, have at it."

He pouted. "I tried once. He didn't even get offended, just said he's not like that but he hopes I'll find someone special. Of all the nerve!"

Talicia burst out laughing. "You're mad because he wasn't grossed out?"

"I don't know. I'm used to…well, not him. If he wasn't using you, I might like him."

"You *act* like you like him."

"Nope, I refuse." Tyjon raised his chin, and she shook her head, deciding she'd never understand him. He had his own logic, and sometimes it changed by the second. Everything in Tyjon's world depended on his whims.

"I'm sorry you don't like me, Ty."

They both started, and Talicia whirled around to face the doorway. "Stefan, when did you wake up? He didn't mean it like that. Tell him, Ty."

Her brother stuttered and struggled with the burning bacon. Stefan moved past Talicia, tapping her gently on the ass as he did so and took the pan from Tyjon. He salvaged the bacon and added more to the pan.

"You know how to cook?" Tyjon mumbled.

"I do own a restaurant."

"But you're not one of the chefs."

"Tyjon," Talicia snapped.

His eyes widened. "What? He's not."

"Someone close to me is a chef," Stefan explained, "and she taught us all a couple things. Watching her create is an experience. Just sit down and relax. I'll take care of everything."

"Do you, boyfriend," Tyjon said and dropped into a chair to cross one leg over the other.

Talicia sat as well and watched Stefan move about the kitchen. He brought out various items from the refrigerator and set them on the counter. Once she had to pop up and move the toaster and the blender to another spot so he could have counter space. Their kitchen wasn't but so big, and three people occupying it at once was a little much.

She wondered who he meant when he said someone close to him was a chef. Why didn't he just say who? Did that mean she was a girlfriend? Sure, he said they would see only each other, but what did it mean in the grand scheme of things? They were secret lovers on his part. That meant he could have anyone in his bed back home.

Jealousy wasn't an emotion Talicia liked to deal with, so she jammed it down and turned her thoughts to other things. The date was drawing closer for when her other partner would show up out of nowhere. She had to be mentally prepared. Come to think of it, Kevin had never come around when Stefan was there, which was good. She didn't want the two to meet. There would be too much drama.

"Here we go," Stefan announced, setting dishes on the table. "I think I overdid it since Shada taught us based on all the staff. Just give me a figure, and I'll leave the money for groceries."

"Oh, hell," Tyjon groaned and grabbed a slice of bacon. "He did not say that."

Talicia narrowed her eyes at him. "What, you think I can't afford food?"

Stefan looked at her in confusion. "Clearly that's not the case since you're a business owner, and I've seen the club packed with customers."

Her anger fizzled as fast as it surfaced. "Oh."

He winked. "What I meant was I wasted your food, and it's only fair I replace it. This meal won't taste as good as leftovers."

"Tyjon's the only one that cooks around here, and it's just me and him. He's hardly ever home, so trust me those leftovers will come in handy when I get hungry tonight. They don't have to be gourmet."

His gaze slid over her figure, and she saw the fire ignite there. Talicia rolled her eyes. *Don't even think about it. I'm sore.*

He appeared to read her mind and sighed. "I'll get Jerome."

They scattered about the living room eating. Talicia noticed Jerome ate enough for three people, and Stefan wasn't a picky eater either. Well, they were some big men. They needed a lot to keep those muscles going. Still, Stefan hadn't exaggerated about cooking a lot. She found herself wondering again about who Shada was and about the restaurant business. Was it fun? Was it fast-paced and exciting like her club?

Stefan followed her into the kitchen to do the dishes. She rinsed while he piled dishes into the washer. "You seem comfortable in this small apartment. I imagine a billionaire lives in a mansion with servants."

"Are you interested in knowing more about my life?"

She sighed. "You always ask me a question when I ask you anything. Never mind."

He straightened and drew her into his arms. "I'll tell you whatever you want to know."

Talicia hesitated. If she asked him, there would need to be an equal exchange of information. As usual, she let the subject drop. "Are you staying another night?"

"I might be persuaded." He kissed her, and she nuzzled closer to him.

"Stay."

"For you, I will."

CHAPTER FOUR

Stefan picked up the report for the fourth time. The numbers swam before his eyes, and he rubbed them. He set the sheet down and stretched, then picked it up again. Sure, he understood for the most part what he was seeing. He wasn't a total idiot, and he'd gotten decent grades while in school. The problem was his interest. Why the hell did Creed have to force these stupid reports onto them every month, expecting them to go over the figures? Then to make matters more of a snorefest, his oldest brother wanted to discuss profits and losses.

Creed knew what type of man Stefan was. He didn't consider himself to be irresponsible exactly, but he wasn't the stuffed shirt type to remain stuck behind a desk either. The best idea he and his other brother Damen had was to purchase their restaurant, Marquette's. Stefan loved it. He enjoyed spending almost every night serving their guests. On the special nights when he got to replace the regular entertainment, he thrilled in it. Music was his heart and soul.

He grinned thinking about how he'd once wanted to pursue a full-time career as a musician. Creed and Damen never discouraged him, but he was pretty sure they hated the idea. Their father had been a total waste of talent, and had neglected them and their mother as they grew up. His brothers didn't want him to fall to the same fate. Stefan didn't believe he would, but his life had taken a different turn anyway, and he didn't regret it.

Voices outside his office door caught his attention, and Stefan welcomed the interruption. He set the papers aside and walked over about to open the door. His bodyguard's words gave him pause.

"Why are you asking me about Stefan?" Jerome said.

"Not so loud, damn it," Pete snapped. "Is he in there?"

"No."

Jerome lied because he already knew where Stefan was. He always knew. Stefan found it annoying his bodyguard could lie with a straight face. Yet, it worked in this situation. As far as Stefan knew Jerome didn't lie to him. Jerome was too blunt for that, but that's the way he liked the man. Stefan might be impulsive, but what kept him from ruining himself and his brothers was the fact that he was an absolute excellent judge of character. He could read a person with just a bit of conversation.

"Well?" Pete pushed. "I have to tell Mr. Creed something. Where's your boss been disappearing to the last few months?"

"I know you guys have all gotten close, and maybe you talk," Jerome said. "That's not me."

"What are you talking about? I would never betray Mr. Creed."

"Yeah, well why do you expect me to tell you Stefan's business?"

"I just thought maybe it wasn't that much of a secret and maybe Mr. Creed hesitated to ask him directly."

Jerome laughed. "Now, I know you lying, bruh. Mr. Creed's not scared of anybody, and he thinks he's the biggest dog in this family. He would have just asked Stefan where he was going."

Stefan had to suppress his own laugh at that point. Just as he thought, Jerome was always blunt and direct. At his words, Pete made a sound of irritation, but he was stubborn. He refused to accept that Jerome wouldn't give up any information. After all, their bodyguards were trained to deal with any situation, including being pressed for intel on Stefan and his brothers. One of the other guards questioning him was a walk in the park.

Stefan thought of how he had slipped away from Jerome that one night to go to the club he had found out about. He should have trusted Jerome, but Jerome had ways of locating him, a simple way like tracking his phone. That knowledge still embarrassed Stefan when he thought back to it. Still, nothing had happened to him, and Jerome had stood off stage watching while he performed an audition.

That same night, Stefan met Talicia. For a moment, he forgot about the conversation going on outside his office door to recall the night he met her.

"Talicia Clay." She stuck out her hand, all business and serious. "You'll be the third to go on. Just give the band your music. They know practically every song in existence, and if not, they can wing it."

Her strong grip had surprised him in a woman so tiny. She was built small and petite. He'd had to look down at her, but the way she raised her chin, almost in defiance and with the spark of anger in her eyes, he'd been intrigued.

"Stefan," he'd responded and held onto her hand. Her eyes widened a touch, and then he saw the anger flare hotter. She tried to crush his fingers to let him know she wouldn't go for any tricks. Stefan had only smiled. In the end, she jerked away. The men around her gave him dirty looks, but he ignored them. Talicia didn't appear to be overly aware of them either, as if she didn't see that they cared about her.

While Stefan waited for his turn to audition, he watched Talicia. Dressed in a staid business suit that hardly bumped out at the chest area, she didn't appear very feminine. In fact, he was sure she didn't wear a stitch of makeup. Her hair was styled with short tight curls, but it was the big brown eyes that drew his gaze so often.

Stefan saw something in Talicia he didn't see often—a woman strong and hard on the outside but vulnerable on the inside. He had met plenty of women who had strong characters built by the hard knocks of life. Talicia wasn't one of those. He would stake his life on it. She had built herself up on the outside to give the imitation of being something she wasn't.

"Stefan, are you ready?" Talicia had called, and moved in front of him. He stared at her. She'd removed her jacket, and now he got a better view of her body. Thin but toned arms and small breasts that would feel nice under his palms. His cock stirred seeing her up close, but he cleared his throat and straightened in his chair. Good thing the club was dark. He didn't want to offend her.

"I'm ready," he said and rose to his feet. Damn, she was so tiny he could probably lift her with one arm. He'd like to try.

She glared at him, mouth tight, as if she read his mind. "Are you sure you want to do this? You're not exactly the type to like or play our kind of music."

"All music is my type," he assured her. "If you have a problem with me being white…"

"Don't be stupid." She gestured. "Look around, we got a few. Sure, they grew up around black people and think a tan will fool somebody, but whatever. To each his own."

He chuckled. "I'm happy with who I am. I just want to play and sing. If I can entertain some, all the better."

She folded her arms over her chest, drawing her blouse tighter to those lovely breasts. "You have to impress me. Nobody else."

He'd leaned way down toward her beautiful upturned face, and just when she grew startled like he would kiss her, he shifted his aim to the side and whispered in her ear. "I'll do whatever you want to please you."

"Don't even," she growled, but Stefan had spun away and performed just for her. By the time the night was over, he had her under him, and the two of them made love all night.

Of course, Stefan knew his impulsive proposal the next morning was crazy. Even crazier was slipping away from Jerome again after he proposed to Talicia. However, it wasn't the first time he'd jumped over the edge to see where it got him. Not marriage though. This was a new frontier, and even he admitted to himself he'd crossed all lines. That was one of the reasons he kept his marriage to Talicia a secret from his family.

Stefan sighed and came back to the present. He returned to his seat with the report as Jerome finished his conversation with Creed's bodyguard and stepped into his office. "Stefan, did you hear?"

"Yes." He saw no reason to lie. "I appreciate you keeping my secret." Jerome knew Talicia was his lover but not his wife.

"That's my job, and as far as I'm concerned it's none of their business what you do. So what you're Stefan

Marquette. It doesn't mean you shouldn't have privacy."

Stefan chuckled. "Thanks. No one's harassing you, are they?"

Jerome rolled his shoulders. "Don't worry about it. I got you, and these are some pretty big shoulders should anyone get stupid enough to challenge me."

"I doubt that will happen."

Stefan shook his head, amused. He hadn't chosen Jerome for the color of his skin but for his skill. Yet, as an African American, Jerome fit into Talicia's club a lot better than he did. Stefan liked the man a lot and considered him somewhat to be a friend. He'd encouraged Jerome to call him Stefan and drop the mister. All the other guards stuck to a more formal address to his brothers and their significant others. Stefan did make sure Jerome stuck with Ms. Talicia for his wife as he never wanted Talicia to feel less than what she was.

"I'm not sure how much longer I'll be going over there," Stefan said. "The gig might be ending soon."

Jerome nodded and took the seat Stefan indicated. "I guess that's how it goes. You'll get another one, but this time don't sneak off and leave me behind. You can trust me to have your back."

"I know." Stefan talked about the performance, but what he thought about was his marriage. In the beginning, he intended to annul their marriage. In fact, at the time, he couldn't believe he stayed so single-minded to have gone through with it or that Talicia had been carried along to say I do.

Their wedding night, he'd made love to her, and it was then he realized the fever she had started. He couldn't stop touching her, kissing her, listening to her. Even in the club, he watched how she ran the place, with precision Creed could be proud of. Yet, she was always tense and on guard. The only time she relaxed was when he had her in bed. Then he worked to make sure she experienced intense pleasure. Not to mention his own.

Visit after visit, he told himself they would break it off and just dissolve the marriage. Yet, he knew the time for annulment was past. Now they were looking at the only way to break the connection being through divorce.

No, his mind shouted. If he gave Talicia a divorce, she would end the affair. He wasn't ready for that to happen. Therefore, no divorce. Period. Stefan knew she wanted him, and his desire for her hadn't lessened one iota in almost a year. If anything it had grown, along with his feelings for her. He couldn't say for sure if he loved her. They spent so little time in each other's presence, and when they did, it was all about lovemaking.

Even now, thinking about her, he got a hard-on. He wished he could see her more often, but his schedule didn't allow it, and neither did hers. They were from two different worlds, and he doubted the two would ever meet. She didn't want to come to him, and he wasn't sure his family would accept her without hurting her first. No, he refused to allow them the chance. Talicia was far more vulnerable than she believed or anyone around her knew.

Maybe I'm being selfish. Am I embarrassed over her?

He thought about Talicia and didn't think so. She was intelligent and successful. For the most part, she ran the club on her own, handled the finances, the management, hiring, marketing, customer service, all the various parts he and his brothers shared. If anything, he admired what she had done. Aside from all that, she was so damn sexy he wanted to make love to her on a nightly basis.

Would it be so bad if he pushed to get her to come to him? To reveal her existence to his family? He and she could get to know each other, and maybe the sexual relationship could become something that resembled the beautiful couple that Damen and Heaven were and that Creed and Shada strove to be.

No, he didn't want to be tied down, stuck in one place. Not that he desired multiple women. From the first night he met Talicia, he'd been faithful to her. The idea of a steady marriage like what his brothers enjoyed also smacked of staying put. He was known for dropping everything and flying off wherever he wanted, whenever the mood struck him. So far, he'd hung around New Orleans and the restaurant. He loved it, but that might change tomorrow.

With a wife and maybe later a baby, he would be looking at a very different life. He was thirty-one. There was plenty of time to go until he settled down—if he did. Stefan recognized his impulse to marry Talicia had been partially driven by seeing how nuts Creed was over Shada. Then he had stumbled upon a black woman, found her irresistible, and suggested marriage. Creed would kill him if he found out. His older brother was somewhat of a bully as well, so he might hurt Talicia. Not physically, but emotionally. No, they were better as they were now. If in a few months, she pushed for a divorce, he would allow it. For now, he would hold onto her and enjoy the limited time they shared.

"You there, boss?"

Jerome's voice pulled him from his thoughts. "Yeah, I'm here. Listen, I'm probably going to go back again soon. I'll rearrange my schedule. I'm also going to make it a longer visit. I might take Talicia shopping somewhere or on a trip."

"I can make the arrangements if you don't want to ask your secretary in New York."

Stefan hesitated. He'd depended on Jerome to arrange

trips when he wanted to keep Creed out of the loop of his actions. Their corporate secretaries didn't have the loyalty of his bodyguard, not when it came to Creed. "No, not yet. I have to talk to her about it. I'll give her a call first. I just wanted to give you a head's up."

"All right then. Just let me know when you're ready."

A knock sounded on the door, and Stefan called out for the person to enter. Jerome made himself scarce. Damen stuck his head around the door. "Just checking to see if you've fallen asleep yet."

"Haha, funny." Stefan grinned and stood. "I'm glad you interrupted. Those numbers were beginning to blur."

"I say we ditch the reports. Our shifts are starting anyway. There have been some interesting visitors of late."

Stefan raised an eyebrow at his brother. "You're a married man now. The patrons shouldn't interest you."

Damen twisted the ring on his finger. "They don't, not in that way. Trust me, I love my wife. Heaven is....well, heaven. I'm the luckiest man on earth to have her. Damn, just talking about her makes me want to go find her and trap her in my office for a couple hours."

Stefan knew exactly what his brother meant, but he didn't say so. "Since she doesn't work at Marquette's that would be quite a trip for a quickie."

"I said a couple hours, man. No way can I accept a quickie with Heaven. You'll know what I mean when you find the one."

Stefan kept silent and scratched the back of his head. He hadn't learned how not to look guilty when it was hinted around about him getting married or as Damen had said, "finding the one." So far, his brothers were so distracted with their own love lives, they never noticed.

"I know," Damen said. "For old times sake, you and I

will case the restaurant, and I'll help you pick out a beauty that should rock your world tonight. I'm pretty good at spotting them."

"I'm sure you are," Stefan said, "but no thanks. I can choose my own lovers."

"Come on, man." Damen slung an arm about Stefan's shoulders and propelled him toward the door. "Don't ruin my fun."

"*Your* fun?"

Damen yanked the office door open, and they stepped into the hall. "Yeah, choosing a woman for you. None of us have ever seen your lovers. I mean you charm the ladies better than anyone I know, but I can't remember seeing you leave with them."

"That's because I don't advertise a lady's private affairs."

Damen snorted. "Always the gentleman. Are you even related to us?"

"Leave him alone, Damen," Duke boomed from the other end of the hall. "Who knows? He might be gay and just too scared to come out of the closet. Don't worry, little cousin. I accept you just the way you are."

At Stefan's side, Damen stiffened. He and Duke had never gotten along, and Damen respected Duke even less after he found out Creed had been bailing Duke out of trouble for years without telling them.

"I'm not gay," Stefan assured him.

Duke slapped him on the opposite shoulder, and Damen stepped farther away from the two of them, glaring at their cousin. Duke appeared oblivious to how much Damen disliked him. He always wore a smile, and from the stories that Stefan had heard Duke was more impulsive than he could ever be. The difference lay in the fact that Duke didn't care if he broke the law or endangered his or anyone else's lives.

"You're still in town?" Damen growled. "When are you leaving?"

"I'm here to stay." Duke set his fists on his hips, and Stefan flashed on the image of a swashbuckling pirate. In a way, Duke resembled one. At least he had trimmed the beard and gotten a haircut. The family resemblance was there. He could be Damen's twin, which probably pissed Damen off all the more. "I like Marquette's, and there are too many single women coming through here to leave after a few days."

"Our restaurant isn't your dating service," Damen bit out between gritted teeth. Never mind that he'd just been suggesting to Stefan that he look over the guests for a date. "Why don't you go find a job?"

"Ah, but I have."

Suspicion rose in Damen's gaze, and Stefan knew what was coming.

Duke wiggled his eyebrows. "Tonight, I start as one of the hosts. I told Creed a waiter might be a little much to begin with, and cooking's not my thing."

"You mean the less work involved the better," Damen interrupted.

"Hey, I'm willing to start out at the bottom."

Damen cursed. "I don't expect you to last the week. Before five days, you'll find some reason to quit, or you just won't show up. That's your M.O., isn't it? If you think we're going to support you just because you're family you can forget it."

At last the smile left Duke's face, and he moved closer to Damen. The two men stood chest to chest, nostrils flared. "You've got a big mouth on you, Damen. Don't forget who used to wipe your nose when you were a kid."

"Not you," Damen shot back.

"Yeah, me. Creed wasn't always around. I cleaned up after you when you were bullied."

"Guys, cool it," Stefan tried, but they ignored him.

Damen shoved the other man. "Get out of my face, Duke. You should have never come back from the army. Oh wait, they kicked you out. That's right. I forgot."

"Fuck you!"

Damen surprised Stefan when he threw the first swing. His middle brother hated violence, yet Duke pissed him off so much, he couldn't resist. Stefan watched in shock as Duke deliberately stepped into the swing and let it connect with his jaw. His head snapped back, and he grinned in amusement.

"Wow, you hit like a girl, Damen. Guess your lady wears the pants in your house."

Stefan gasped. "Duke, stop."

Damen roared and launched himself at Duke. This time, their cousin sidestepped him and grabbed Damen's fist, twisted it, and grabbed his brother by the back of the neck. Damen landed on the floor, but he was big enough to unsettle Duke's stance. Duke thumped a shoulder against the wall. Several shouts of surprise rang through the hall, and Stefan looked up to find the entire kitchen staff and the wait staff gathered to watch the fight.

Stefan reached out and grabbed Duke's shoulder. "Let him up, and stop fighting, Duke."

"He thinks he can take me," Duke shot back. "Come on, Damen. Get up if you can."

A door banged. Stefan found himself shouldered aside, and Creed appeared. His oldest brother jerked Duke away from Damen and slammed him against the wall. "What the fuck are you doing inside my restaurant, Duke, with our guests about to arrive and the staff watching?"

Duke sagged, wincing at the pain he must feel in his back. "Uh, having a little fun?"

Stefan held out a hand to help Damen to his feet. Damen took it with reluctance, his face red and glasses askew. Stefan figured Duke had humiliated him, and the relationship had gotten that much worse between them.

"Fun?" Creed snapped. He glanced down the hall. "Back to work!"

The employees scrambled to obey. Creed pointed to Damen and Duke.

"In my office now."

Stefan followed. He was the last inside and shut the door. The space they had originally shared before his and Damen's offices were constructed was spacious, but with four big men in it, he felt a bit cramped. He took up a spot in the far corner and listened to the proceedings.

"Creed, I don't understand how you can give this bum a job," Damen complained. "He's never going to be serious, and frankly, he doesn't deserve it."

Creed parked on the edge of his desk, arms folded over a chest swollen with his suppressed rage. "Whether he deserves it or not, he's family. We never abandon family."

"Oh come on. There's a limit to how much you let him use you."

"No, there's a limit to my patience," Creed growled. "You talk about the restaurant like you care about it, but then I find you fighting in front of the employees."

"What the hell makes you think I started it?"

"Because Duke's all mouth unless you come at him. Are you saying you *didn't?*"

Damen swore and pushed his hands into his hair. Stefan marveled at his oldest brother. Creed was pretty good at knowing all three of them. If he didn't have anger issues, he could probably do everything that Stefan did. Stefan had always admired Creed's strength and his steel will. Yet, he also knew Creed's huge heart and his unwavering loyalty to family. Creed loved family like nothing else. Stefan could have told Damen there wasn't anything Duke could do except maybe hurt Shada that would make Creed abandon Duke.

"He pissed me off," Damen admitted after a few minutes.

"I liked the way you were before, Damen," Creed said. "Since you married Heaven, you seem more apt to physical defense. Do you think she'd like that?"

Damen's eyes widened. "You're lecturing me?"

"Answer the question."

"Fine, I get it, but you can't tell me you trust Duke."

"Trust him? Hell no."

"Hey, cuz, that's cold." Duke seemed more amused than offended.

"You're a screw-up, Duke," Creed said. "We both know it, and I'm going to ride your ass until you get it together. I'll come to your place and drag you out of bed if you even think of missing a day of work. And if you try that shit again you pulled in the hall, I'll make you sorry. See if I go down as easily as Damen."

Duke held up hands in surrender. "Gotcha. I'll keep my nose clean from here on."

Both Creed and Damen looked doubtful, and Stefan had to admit he felt the same. He doubted Duke was ready to reform, but like Creed he had a lot of hope that it would come one day. He agreed with Creed that Duke could learn a lot about taking responsibility for his life, but he also liked Duke's carefree spirit.

Creed's gaze shifted from their brother and Duke to

him, and Stefan straightened. His oldest brother frowned at him. "Stefan, I want to talk to you."

"Uh, later." He zipped to the door and grabbed the knob. "Our shift is starting."

"Fine, tonight after closing." Creed called after him, but Stefan kept moving. He would use the rest of the night to think about how he would put off Creed's questions. Under no circumstances would he tell the man Damen called The Bear about his wife.

CHAPTER FIVE

Stefan's fingers raced over the ivories, and his heart beat faster as the scale climbed higher. He leaned forward, shut his eyes, and leaned back again with the rhythm pulsing through his being. The cheers commenced on the last note, along with enthusiastic clapping in one particular corner. He checked and started to find Tyjon grinning back at him.

Stefan scanned Marquette's, and he came upon Damen's curious gaze and then Duke's knowing one. His cousin grinned big and then looked pointedly at Tyjon. The man actually thought he was gay. Stefan didn't care one way or another. He doubted Damen or Creed would cut him out of their lives if he were gay. The fact that Tyjon was Talicia's brother did concern him. He had never visited the restaurant before tonight.

Tyjon wore some type of glossy material slacks that clung to his hips and thighs and a long-sleeve shirt with a white panel at the front and golden floral print along the sides and sleeves. As was his style, he stood out in the crowd. Even if he dressed more conservatively, Stefan was sure the man would be seen. His big personality radiated in a room. Tyjon could be a performer, but it seemed he had no interest in doing anything other than finding a boyfriend. Stefan knew Talicia had spoiled her brother from their interactions together when he visited.

When his set ended, Stefan prepared to rise, but Tyjon and a beautiful brunette rushed toward the piano to head him off. He sank down on the stool once more and smiled a greeting. Tyjon beat the woman by a few inches and rolled his eyes at her.

"Uh-uhn, boo boo, he's mine. Get lost."

The woman's cheeks pinked.

"Don't be rude," Stefan admonished him. "Hello, I hope you enjoyed the food and the music."

She held out a hand to him, one already holding a slip of paper carrying her number. Then she eyed Tyjon. "Give me a call when you get the chance, Stefan. I'd love to talk about your music."

Tyjon made a rude noise, poking his lips out. "His music, yeah, I'm sure that's what you want you from him."

"Well, neither do you," she snapped and stomped away.

Tyjon chuckled. "I have to give it to her. Girlfriend had backbone. Whatever."

"Ty, what are you doing here?" Stefan cast his voice low but kept a pleasant expression on his face as if Ty was a stranger.

Tyjon glanced around the restaurant, taking in the chandeliers, the landscapes on the walls of an age long gone, and the expanse of white tablecloth-covered tables. "I wanted to see what it was like since I know my sis won't come. She doesn't know what she's missing. This place is bougie, way fancier than the club. Plus people dress up to eat. They crazy."

"You're dressed up," Stefan said, amused.

Tyjon snapped his fingers and spun left and right as if Stefan had asked him to model. "I know, right? I read on your website that there's a dress code. I refused to wear a tie, and they actually gave me one at the door. Can you believe it? I chose this red one because the others were ugly and clashed with my outfit."

"Stefan, who's your friend?" Duke strode up and clapped a heavy hand on Tyjon's shoulder.

Stefan opened his mouth to speak, but Tyjon cut him off. He dipped a hip in Duke's direction and raised his chin, lashes fluttering. "I'm Tyjon. I heard about this restaurant and the yummy men that work here. I wasn't disappointed. So, um, you got a boyfriend?"

Duke smiled bigger. "No, but I'm not looking."

"Not into guys or just not looking right now?"

"I love women too much to switch sides." Duke shrugged. "But Stefan might be interested."

"Stefan isn't gay." Tyjon said it with too much assurance and then bit his lip. Stefan suppressed a groan.

Duke eyed Tyjon and then Stefan. "You happen to know?"

Tyjon stuttered. "I mean, my gaydar knows these things. I'm never wrong."

"But you thought I was a minute ago." Duke's color rose, and Stefan laughed, relaxing a little.

"I think you bruised my cousin's ego, Ty. Let him off the hook." Stefan could kick himself for using Tyjon's nickname just now, but Duke in his annoyance didn't appear to have noticed. He vowed to be more careful and was grateful to Tyjon for not revealing their connection. Tyjon keeping the secret surprised him, especially because Tyjon had admitted he didn't like Stefan. Perhaps he did so to protect his sister, who was more important than either of them.

"Well, damn, why can't a guy have a little fun?" Tyjon complained. "I hoped you were in the mood to try something different. What's your name, big boy? I won't give up hope just yet."

Duke laughed. "It's Duke, and nothing doing. A soft body is all I need. In fact, I see something interesting over there. Later, guys. Have fun."

Stefan watched his cousin walk away, pretty sure that Duke still thought he was gay. He had no idea how the man clung to the notion. Maybe he just wanted to for his own entertainment. Stefan wouldn't put it past Duke to come to such a decision. Duke liked to get his enjoyment at other people's expense. Stefan didn't believe he was mean-spirited, just self-absorbed when it came to what he desired.

"So." Tyjon leaned on the piano and played with a few keys. "I really came to spy on you to see if you have a wife back home who doesn't know about you sneaking off."

"I assure you I don't, and I would prefer to keep things separate, if you know what I mean."

Tyjon frowned. "That's what I figured. Why don't you just break up with her? My sister deserves a man who loves her and isn't ashamed of her."

Stefan clenched his jaw. "I'm not ashamed."

"Oh no? So letting that guy who just walked away think you're gay is better than letting him know you're slumming with my sister? That's not shame at all?"

Stefan shut the piano top harder than he meant to. Creed, who had just walked into the dining room, glanced his way. Damn, he'd hoped to leave before Creed found him. He wasn't scared or intimated by Creed, but he didn't want to have the discussion about his personal life.

All the same, Stefan willed Creed's gaze to remain on him. Instead, it slipped over to Tyjon. Unlike Duke, Creed didn't look like he questioned Stefan's manhood. Yet, one never knew. When he wasn't angry, Creed knew how to maintain a poker face. He wouldn't have done so well in business if he couldn't.

"Ty," Stefan said in a low tone, "I understand you're concerned about your sister, but what she and I have is our business. The terms are what we agreed on."

"She likes you. Of course she would agree. You rich guys always call the shots on how you use us. I had a boyfriend with money once. He wasn't rich as you, but he owned some vacation real estate and drove fancy cars. I was told not to come by his house. He had an apartment downtown. Come to find out he was married to a woman!"

Tyjon's mouth hardened.

"I don't do men on the down low. I believe in being who you are and doing what you want. If you were such a good guy, you wouldn't hide my sister in a closet."

"You're right," Stefan said.

Tyjon blinked. "What?"

"I'm wrong for how I treat her."

"Are you pulling some reverse psychology on me, because it won't work."

"No, I'm not." Stefan stood. "I should bring her around here, but right now I'm not going to."

Tyjon's eyes widened.

"I'm being honest with you. So you have a choice. You can go over there and tell my brothers the truth, or you can let Talicia decide what she wants to do about me. I'm not prepared to let her go. Not yet. She's mine as long as she agrees to it."

"You're that into her?"

"Yeah," Stefan admitted, smiling. "I'm that into her."

Tyjon made a rude noise. "If you were, you'd marry her."

"I would, wouldn't I?" Stefan snorted. "So what's it going to be?"

"I'm not betraying my sister. Don't think I'd do it for you." Tyjon groaned. "Why do you have to be so pretty and with that voice? I hate you, but I don't. Get it?"

"Yes, I get it. I'll work harder to make you like me."

Tyjon waved a hand at him, for some reason reminding Stefan of Talicia. The two of them looked so much alike, even more so now that Talicia had cut her hair shorter. Hers was straight and slicked to her head, and her brother's lay in tight curls. All the same, Stefan saw the differences. Tyjon behaved in a much more feminine way than Talicia, but Stefan had experienced the genuine womanliness that was his wife. Damn, there he went again, thinking about her, which led to craving her. He would need to make that phone call soon and hope she agreed to take a trip with him.

"Well, I'm going," Tyjon told him. "I'm glad I came though. I always thought of you just playing elevator music here, but it was all right. And you added a little funk to that last song, didn't you? Learned that at our club."

Stefan winked. "The guests seemed to like it."

"Yeah, they did. You can't beat our music. So anyway, do me a favor, Stefan."

"What's that?"

He hesitated. "Don't tell Talicia I came by, okay? She'd get all mad and tell me to keep my nose out of her business."

"Really?"

"Yeah, really. Don't give me that look." Tyjon

pouted. "I have to take care of my sister. I'm still the man in our family, and there's no one else to do it."

Stefan was tempted to ask about their parents or other family members but changed his mind. If Talicia didn't share her background with him, he wouldn't know. He respected her enough to accept it if she never told him the details.

"I won't say anything," he promised Tyjon. "You do me a favor too."

"I know, I know. Call first." Tyjon blew him kisses and laughed. Then he turned and left the restaurant. He'd done it on purpose, leaving before Stefan could ask him not to come. Yet, even as Stefan thought about it, he doubted he could have formed the words. Forbidding Talicia or her family from coming to him seemed far too wrong to accept, even if it meant revealing their secret.

"Who was that?" Creed asked as he walked up.

"A fan of music." Stefan didn't lie.

Creed narrowed his eyes at him. "I know you, Stefan, and I can tell when you're keeping something from me."

"Come on, big bro," Stefan said, doing a good imitation of Damen. "Don't you trust me?"

"No." Creed folded his arms, frowning. "Do you know the number of problems you've lumped onto my head in the last decade? Scratch that, all your life."

"Where would the excitement be if I didn't bring it to you, Creed? You're a guy who plays it safe and calculates every move."

His brother grunted in protest, but he didn't deny Stefan's claim in words. "I'm not going to get into your business, but just promise me you're not about to get into another venture."

Stefan widened his grin and held up three fingers as if he made a solemn Boy Scout promise. Creed's doubt radiated. "Well, even if you were, let me warn you. Damen isn't liable to go along with it now that he's married, and you need two signatures to sign off on anything."

Just because he could rile his brother, Stefan rocked on his heels. "I'm a persuasive guy. I can convince Damen of anything."

"Stefan!"

He burst out laughing. "All right, Creed. Just relax. I'm not buying anything. In fact, I was thinking it was getting kind of quiet in my life right now. A vacation might do me some good, take time off for a little while."

"I thought you liked New Orleans. We've hardly been here a year. Are you getting tired of it already? Wait, what am I saying? Of course you are. You never did stay still for long."

"I said a vacation," he reiterated. Creed's assumption had him considering moving away, choosing a new city to live in, a new venture. He found the thought didn't sit as well as it would have before Marquette's and before the gig at the club. He would never be a sensation on the stage and have millions of records selling, but he wasn't sure he wanted that dream anymore. Okay, maybe a little. The bug would never die, which was why he still performed.

Stefan's assurance settled his brother down some. "I don't have to give you permission to take a vacation. You're part owner of the restaurant."

Stefan patted Creed's cheek, amused. "I wasn't asking for permission."

"What was I thinking? You never do."

"Anyway, it's still up in the air." Stefan brushed a hand over the back of his head. "I have to sort some things out first to be sure."

"Sounds like you're wrestling over something. I've never seen you think so hard about a decision. Normally, you're gone, and I get a post card after the fact."

"Don't be dramatic, Creed. I don't send post cards."

Creed had to laugh. "You know what I mean. I think I feel teary. My brothers are growing up."

"Now that's a good joke. I feel like I have to prove you wrong."

"Don't try too hard. I've got a baby on the way, and I want to concentrate on my wife. Come to think of it, I need to get into the kitchen to make sure she's not taking over again. I told her not to stand too long on her feet. We hired the extra chef to relieve a lot of her duties."

"Good luck with making that work. You know Shada better than that."

Creed grumbled as he walked away, but Stefan wasn't worried about him and Shada. Since she had calmed down about the baby, she had set a date for their wedding. In another month, they were going to be married.

Everyone had been looking at Stefan, talking about when he would find someone. Being the youngest of the three brothers, they had said, it was fitting he was last. He hadn't corrected them to let any of them know he was the first, not the last. His marriage to Talicia happened before Heaven even showed up in the restaurant and eventually married Damen. If Stefan were honest with himself, he would admit a small concern niggled at the back of his mind. Would he be the first also to introduce divorce to their family?

CHAPTER SIX

Stefan left the restaurant and slid into the back seat of his car. As was his custom, Jerome drove. Stefan sat deep in thought as they headed toward the Garden District and his home. When they were close to the drive, Jerome activated the button to open the wrought iron gate. Also, like usual, Stefan felt his mouth tighten. He liked his house but hated the barrier to get onto the grounds. Somehow it felt like he cut off the world from having access to him and vice versa. He loved being around people, and the gate gave the wrong message.

"I see that look," Jerome said, watching him in the rearview with a grin. "You know it's necessary, Stefan. Gotta keep you safe. Your brothers had fences put up too."

"I don't have to like it."

"People get stupid, and it's easier on us to look out for you if we have the extra security."

"You're right. I apologize. I don't want to add to your burden."

"You're not a burden. Plus going to the other side of town…"

"No one has ever followed me over here."

Jerome swiped a thumb across his nose. "That's because of my driving skills. Seriously though, it's possible, so we have to be careful. For the most part, even though you and your brothers are famous, everybody seems to love you. We haven't had any major issues. I want to keep it that way."

"Got it," Stefan assured him.

He knew what Jerome said was true. While Stefan and his brothers ran Marquette's, a small venture compared to their parent company's holdings, they were billionaires. Creed might get onto him about purchasing out of the parent company's funds, but his personal bank account could support with ease anything he chose to do. What he enjoyed most of all was spending time with his brothers. The last decade or more had been a great ride because Creed and Damen were with him.

As Jerome pulled up to the front door of his house, Stefan removed his cell phone from his pocket and speed-dialed Talicia. She didn't answer on the first ring, and he tapped the phone against his lips as he considered whether to try again. A check of the time said she was probably still at the club, but he knew she kept her phone in her hand.

He tried a second time, and she answered on the third ring, her voice sharp and low. "I can't talk now."

Stefan didn't hear the usual blaring music in the background. Perhaps she was in her office, but he didn't like the tightness in her tone. "Everything okay?"

"Yes, fine."

"Licia."

She sighed. "Just business. I'll call you later."

Before he could respond, she ended the call. He didn't realize he squeezed his cell too tight in his palm until the cracking sound. After he released the pressure, he checked the face. Thank goodness there was no damage, but now he wondered about Talicia. She had never hung up on him. Not that he called all that often. Most of the time he did so only when he planned to come to the club. He'd also heard tension in her tone before. Business did that to a person. This seemed different, or was he adding issues where there were none because he wanted to see her?

Stefan had spent almost a year wanting her all the time but denying himself except for when he chose to go back to the club. He was used to nights lying in bed, jerking off as he thought of her. Yet, this was the shortest amount of time he had ever spent away and was thinking of going back.

Wait, is that what I'm doing? Going back?

He strode into the house and thought a minute about heading to the kitchen. After a night of serving, he wasn't hungry. Whenever he asked for it, a plate of food was prepared for him, but tonight he hadn't eaten. Instead, he went up to his room and loosened the tie at his throat then unbuttoned his shirt.

The closet door stood open a little, and he spotted the small case he had taken with him to see Talicia. That was different too. Most often, he spent one night with her and just switched into a pair of jeans and a T-shirt the next morning. He kept a few changes of clothing at her place, but nothing fancy. His maid had unpacked for him, but Stefan didn't need the dress clothes cleaned. He never followed through with what he'd planned this time—to take Talicia to dinner.

What was he doing? She had his head in a tailspin. He expected it to end soon, but then he held on. Damn it, if he could think straight when he was around her, everything would be fine.

Stefan stepped into the shower and shut his eyes. He leaned a hand against the back wall and ducked his head beneath the spray. His cock started to harden, but he refused to jerk off. Frustration gripped him because he kept thinking about how Talicia sounded on the phone.

"It's not that big a deal," he tried to convince himself. Then he realized it didn't matter one way or another. He wanted to see her, so he was going back. That's all there was to his mental debate.

"To hell with it." He stepped out of the shower, dried off, and dressed as fast as he could. A stab at the phone on his bedside table activated the intercom system, and he called down to Jerome's room. "Jerome, I know you must be in bed by now, but I need to make a run."

Jerome yawned over the line. "Not a problem. Where are we going?"

Stefan hesitated. "Talicia's."

"Got it."

He waited for a comment on his decision, but it never came. Jerome didn't even hint at his impatience or if he thought Stefan was making a mistake. He knew which lines not to cross, and Jerome had never questioned Stefan on his personal life when it had nothing to do with his job.

A short while later, they were on the road again, and Stefan tapped his leg with a finger, eager to get across town. His entire body and mind felt tight in anticipation of arriving at his destination. When they pulled onto the grounds where Talicia lived with Tyjon, Stefan scanned the lot. He didn't know why he didn't go to the club first since it was early yet, but her car was there. Her apartment was at the back of the complex, so he didn't have a clear view as to whether the lights were on.

"Should I wait?" Jerome asked.

Stefan paused beside the car. Jerome had stepped out with him, and while he spoke to Stefan, his gaze searched the lot constantly.

"Stay with the car," Stefan said. "I'm just going to run up and—"

"Uh, boss, by wait, I meant walk you to her door and then wait. I'm not staying out here without seeing you pass into her place."

Stefan ran fingers through his hair. "Oh, right. Sorry, forgot about that. Yeah, come on. We'll play it by ear."

They started up the stairs, and Stefan picked up the sound of a man's voice. He figured it was a neighbor until Talicia responded. A door opened and closed. He stopped moving. The hall was silent, and none of the neighbors stirred.

"Everything okay?" Jerome asked. He had moved into the building ahead of Stefan, but he paused when Stefan did.

"Yeah."

Stefan continued up until he reached Talicia's door. He raised his hand and hesitated again. In the years he'd been seeing women, he had never allowed himself to obsess over any of them. He enjoyed the pleasures the female body could provide and gave as much as he got. Once or twice, he imagined himself in love, but it never lasted. Not once did it ever interfere with his chosen lifestyle.

Standing outside Talicia's door without warning her he was coming felt like he was checking up on her. Stefan was the trusting type, and even when he did catch a steady lover seeing another man, it hadn't fazed him more than irritation. He'd broken the relationship off. So what was this tightness in his chest tonight at the mere thought that Talicia might have a man in her apartment? He shouldn't have even suspected it just because of her tone of voice, let alone come here.

Jerome waited behind him in total silence, and when Stefan glanced at him, his face showed no emotion at all. Despite that, heat suffused Stefan's face. He was embarrassed this episode had a witness, yet he was used to staff surrounding him and witnessing most of what he and his brothers did.

I could turn around now and leave. She'll never know.

Stefan raised his hand and rapped on the door with his knuckles. Then he chided himself for not ringing the bell like normal. The knock sounded angry. He didn't want to give that impression. Too late, he heard her footsteps approaching and the exclamation when she must have seen his face through the peephole.

The door opened, and he met his wife's gaze. *Guilt.* Stefan read people as if their minds were spread before him. He knew what he saw on Talicia's face, and he stepped by her without asking if he could come in. She stepped back just before his arm brushed hers, and he heard the squeak of her fingers gripping the doorknob.

"Stefan, what are you doing back here so soon? Jero—"

"I'm sorry, Ms. Talicia, but because you're not alone and I don't know who he is, I have to come in with Stefan. I apologize for my intrusion."

Jerome knew better than to apologize for Stefan's.

"It-it's fine," she murmured.

The door clicked shut behind them, but Stefan's attention was all for the man in front of him, the older man with slightly thinning hair, who had taken his shoes off and was swigging noisily from a can of beer and sporting an obvious hard-on. He eyeballed Stefan around the can, nervous and sweating but arrogant. A touch overweight but probably still appealing to women, the African American man wore a tailored suit, which said he had money. A lingering scent of cigars wafted from his direction.

"Who are you?" the man said after he swallowed.

"Stefan." He tried to muster a smile but failed. That was a rare occurrence for him. "You?"

Talicia rushed over to Stefan's side. "Stefan, this is my business partner, Kevin Williams."

Just business, she had said. As far as he knew, Talicia never conducted business at home. Why would she? "Perhaps I've interrupted something."

"No," she began.

"Yes," the man snapped. "Talicia and I were about to have a little conversation."

Stefan raised his eyebrows. "A conversation?"

Talicia glared at the man. "Kevin, don't start crap that doesn't need to be started."

"Where's Tyjon?" Stefan asked.

"He's got a date. Anyway, what are you doing back here? You usually disappear longer. Was there something you needed, another booking? Stop by the club and—"

She must have seen his jaw tighten and let the words die away on her own. He folded his arms over his chest. "I'm more interested in the conversation you and your partner intend to have here at your apartment rather than at the club."

The man laughed and shook the empty can. He held it out to Talicia. "Get me another one, would you, baby?"

"Baby?" Stefan growled.

Talicia swore. She ignored the can and held up her hands to Stefan. "It's not what you think, Stefan. He calls every woman baby. The man's a chauvinist."

Kevin cackled. "Damn, Talicia. You know how to cut a man down, but that's what I like about you. Yeah, I call every woman baby, but you're special."

He sidled over to her and smacked her on the ass. Stefan lost focus for a second, but when he came to himself, he held Kevin up in the air with his feet dangling above the floor. Jerome zipped over to him and touched his arm.

"Boss, I got this," Jerome said.

"No, *I* do." Stefan cracked Kevin across the jaw and sent him falling backward to land on the couch. The softness of the cushions might have broken his fall, but the impact of Stefan's fist knocked him out cold. Stefan spun away from the jackass to face Talicia, and he froze.

She stood before him with her fists raised, feet spread apart, mouth tight. Her eyes were wide with pain and hurt but also with the same determination he had seen a thousand times. All his anger ebbed away.

"If you even think about hitting me," she said through clenched teeth, "I'm going to tell you right now, I can defend myself. I have taken down guys as big as you before."

Stefan's mouth fell open. "I have never nor would I ever hit you. Why would you think that?"

He saw the tears welling, but she widened her eyes to combat them. Her fists were still high, but they wavered. She swallowed several times.

"I don't want to fight you, Stefan, but I will."

He sighed. "Jerome, take him out for me."

"On it." Jerome hauled Kevin over his shoulder.

"Wait a minute," Talicia cried out. "What are you doing? Stefan, you can't just waltz into my apartment and do what you want to. Jerome, put him down."

In her agitation, she dropped her fists, and Stefan

snaked a hand out to grasp her wrist and draw her to him. She struggled in his arms and punched him in the solar plexus. All the breath left his body. He felt like he'd been hit by a prizefighter.

Stefan gritted his teeth and bore it until the door shut behind Jerome and Kevin. Then he released Talicia. Right away, she put space between them, her anger at an all time high.

"I don't like being manhandled."

"I'm your husband."

"Don't even pull that shit. Why did you come back here, and what did you hit him for? You and I are just lovers, and that's all. I told you—"

"I know. It's a piece of paper that we share. You're right, Licia, but I take that paper seriously. I want to know if you've been sleeping with him behind my back."

"No, I haven't." She spun away. He was tempted to drag her back to face him, but his side burned. Damn, the woman was strong.

"Then what was going on tonight? He seemed to think he had a right to touch you."

"He smacked my butt. It's nothing football players haven't done a million times."

"You're not playing ball, and this isn't a field," he snapped.

She faced him. "Why would you believe me? Nothing I say will make a difference."

"Try me."

For a few moments, she said nothing. He almost thought she would ignore him and let him think what he wanted to, but he refused to leave without an explanation. If that meant he had to keep her from rearranging his internal organs with her punch so be it.

She sighed and walked to the dining room to flop

onto a chair. "He asked if he could stay the night."

Stefan ground his teeth.

"Not like that. He had an argument with the ho he brought to his house. The police were called, some drama, and she got to stay, but he had to go. They said something about she'd have trouble finding a place to sleep with the baby, but he would be fine for one night. So he came to me."

"You're home early."

"I drove him over here. The ho apparently busted his windshield too." She rubbed a hand over her face.

"Licia." He moved to stand in front of her. Desire came over him to touch her. No matter what she told him that bastard who wanted Talicia, and Stefan told her so.

"I know, all right?" She stood and wrapped her arms around his waist. "The reason I looked crazy when you came in was because the fool had just tried to come onto me. I was about to beat him down, but you knocked."

Stefan rubbed his side. "I wish you had hit him rather than me."

"I thought you were going to attack me."

"I never have."

"Yeah, but experiences die hard."

He raised her chin, taking in her small build, wide eyes, and soft vulnerable mouth. "Has someone hurt you?"

"Too many to count."

He stiffened, but she patted his chest.

"Easy, Stefan. Not lately. If anyone tried, I wouldn't have stopped with one hit like I did with you. I would have put him in the hospital. Unfortunately, I can't do that with my partner, but he would have felt pain tonight thinking he could grab on me."

Stefan ran a hand over her ass and squeezed. "I don't

want another man touching you or smacking your butt."

She smirked. "I know."

"Licia."

"I hear you, Stefan. Don't worry. I don't have any interest in anyone else."

"And." He hesitated. If he started dictating her actions, she'd be liable to do the opposite just to prove her independence. Yet, he couldn't stop himself from voicing his concern. The memory of that asshole's dick tenting his pants drove Stefan insane. "I don't want him to stay here, not even for a night."

"I know." She laughed at his expression and patted his chest again. "He won't stay ever. I learned my lesson. It gave the fool ideas, but he was drunk. I doubt he'll look at me like that tomorrow when he's sober. Either way, he should have enough money to stay in a hotel if the skank didn't spend it all."

"Thank you." He drew her closer and kissed her lips. "About that punch…"

"I'm sorry. I know you're not the type to hit, but I forgot for a minute. I was so mad because it was like I'd been caught doing something wrong. I'm not the one that was wrong. He was. Stefan, you're my only lover, okay? That's never been an issue with us."

He nodded. "I believe and trust you."

"That punch though. You knocked him out in one blow. He's going to feel it tomorrow."

"I hope he won't start any trouble because of it."

She rolled her eyes. "Let him try and see if I don't give him another experience just the same. I'm not playing with Kevin. I have to put up enough with his stupidity. Coming on to me is way more than I'm willing to take."

"Do you want me to talk to him?"

She stood on her tiptoes and hung her arms about his neck. Stefan encircled her waist and raised her off her feet. Her soft body aligned with his, and his cock swelled. She made a small noise of pleasure that took his desire to the next level, but then she wiggled to get down. With reluctance, he set her on her feet.

"No, I can handle it. Now, are you going to tell me what this visit is about?"

"Come away with me, Talicia, just you and me where no one will get in between us. Where we can enjoy each other's bodies sunup and sundown. Where we can work out what it is that keeps us bound together."

CHAPTER SEVEN

"So are you going to go, sis?" Tyjon asked as he held a compact in his hand and touched up his eye shadow. "I hear Cancun is nice. *I* wouldn't know because my last boyfriend was stingy even though he made all this money."

"Bitter much, Ty?" Talicia hardly paid him any mind. She'd turned the lights lower in the office and watched over the club floor. Tonight, Kevin had come just like she knew he would. She'd thought to convince him to do something other than get on her last nerve. That all changed when he woke up to realize Stefan had knocked his gold tooth loose. He had had to go to the dentist to have it repaired, and it was a good thing she refused to tell him Stefan's last name. The drama wouldn't have ended.

Instead, she had to deal with his pissy attitude because he was embarrassed Stefan got the better of him. She grinned remembering. Yeah, she'd been scared and upset that Stefan was mad at her. Not once in all the time she'd known him had she ever been afraid of his size. He was huge but so excessively sweet. The other night when he thought she was cheating on him, he'd been scary.

Big men like Stefan went down as easy as any of the smaller men. Talicia hadn't spent all that time training her body for nothing. The issue was it was him and how much she loved him. She'd almost cried too. Years had passed since she shed tears, and as much as it hurt loving Stefan and knowing they didn't have a future, she had held in the pain and kept it to herself.

When Stefan realized she thought he was going to hit her, he looked so ashamed. Damn, that's why she loved him. The man never wanted her to be afraid of him. The idea was inconceivable, and all she wanted after that was to be in his arms. Of course, Stefan complicated matters by asking her to go on a trip with him. They had never done anything except drive straight from the club to her apartment. Not one date.

"Well, Licia? Are you going to go away with Stefan or not?"

"Are you worried?"

She squinted, trying to see what Kevin was doing. The bald man he spoke with looked familiar, but she couldn't see his face. Suspicion made her keep watching them, and sure enough it looked like he gave Kevin something.

"I know they're not trading drugs in my club." Talicia charged toward the door, but Tyjon yelped and threw his makeup aside to run after her. He caught her before she could do more than open the door.

"Don't go down there, girl," he begged. "Drug people are crazy dangerous."

"I'm dangerous. Kevin doesn't even try to keep this club going, and he's risking the police coming up in here."

"Then ask him later."

"He'll lie."

"So he's going to tell the truth with the drug dealer right there?"

She hesitated. Her brother was right. Kevin would deny it either way, and she risked pissing off the dealer. Better to point him out and tell the others he wasn't allowed back. If stupid Kevin wanted to do drugs, he could do it on his own time where it wouldn't risk her livelihood.

"This is why I can't stand him," she grumbled. "I wish I could go back in time and say no when he wanted to come in on our plan."

Tyjon shut the door and wandered over to the couch to look for his makeup. Talicia would kill him if he had stained the leather. "We didn't have enough money to start it by ourselves."

She sucked her teeth. "I'd have figured it out one way or another. I always do."

"Yeah, you would do, Licia. You're smart. Don't worry either because Kevin will get bored soon enough and we won't see him for two or three months."

"I'm hoping."

"He's not stupid. He won't risk doing anything too crazy to risk the club."

She eyed her brother.

"Okay, he's not overly stupid. Anyway, who knows? He might really get bored and sell out to us."

"That will never happen. One of his ho's would spend all the money he made in a week. He needs steady income, and this club provides it. I don't see him walking away anytime soon."

"Damn." Tyjon blew a kiss at his reflection in the compact. "What if we ask Jerome to kill him?"

"Tyjon!"

"You think I'm joking? Those guys are killers."

"What guys?"

"Those…uh…" Her brother looked like he was thinking up an excuse. Then his face cleared. "It stands to reason if Stefan has a bodyguard his brothers do. In fact, I saw pictures of them online. There's this whole fan site devoted to the bodyguards. Let me bring it up for you."

"Never mind. I'm not interested."

"Girl, they're huge, except one of them. I want me one."

"Are any of them gay?"

"Who knows, but I'm always willing to convert."

"You or him."

Her brother looked scandalized. "*Him!* You know good and well coochie don't do it for me."

"Don't be gross, Ty. Look, I can't help it. I have to get down there. I just don't feel right if I'm not floor level watching everything. Don't have a conniption. I'm not going to approach Kevin. I'll see you later."

"Wait, Licia. Tell me at least if you're going to go on vacation with Stefan. If you don't, can you give me your ticket?"

Talicia kept walking down the stairs. No sense in answering his outrageous suggestion. The night passed slowly for Talicia because she kept thinking of Stefan. Really, from the moment he asked her to take a vacation with him, she was on board. She'd told him she had to think about it, but days spent with the two of them alone? Hell yes!

They could go wherever she wanted, he'd said, and he would foot the bill. She'd fussed that she could afford to pay her own way, but he had stubbornly refused. Then she pulled the thing about needing time to think about it because she was a busy woman. Sure, she was busy but not so much she couldn't find someone to run the club for a week.

The more she dreamed about it, the more she went through her wardrobe in her head, considering what she would take. Stefan had suggested some place warm, and so had Tyjon. Her on a beach in a bikini was comical, but she wouldn't mind a wrap and a one piece.

Talicia's head was scarcely on the job as she locked the door behind the last person. Then she recalled she needed to recheck the men's bathroom. Some people got notions about hanging out after hours in a bar and getting drunk for free. The bouncers made the rounds, but sometimes they got sloppy. That's why she stayed on them. Talicia pressed a hand to her mouth yawning and stretched the other arm over her head. She looked toward the DJ booth and made a signal. Cut the music. Quiet was what she craved, and her pillow so she could think about the trip.

Just as she was about to go around to the back hall that led to the bathroom, a man stepped out in front of her. She jerked to a stop and frowned. "We're closed, sir."

The bald head, height, and the black dress shirt told her this was the man Kevin had been dealing with earlier. Talicia went on alert and tried to recall if all the bouncers had left. At least the DJ should still be in his booth, and he might be watching right now. He had access to his cell phone and the landline if need be to call the police.

Baldy strolled over to the bar and bent to the side to look under the counter. He pulled out a bottle of vodka and twisted the cap. "I wanted to talk to you about a business proposition."

"I discuss business between five p.m. and two a.m. As I said, we're closed. Now you have five seconds to put that back before I call the police." She preferred not to start out with threatening to beat anyone's ass. As much as she knew how to fight, she didn't like to. Handling things legally was better.

He grinned at her as he set a glass on the counter and began pouring. "You don't want to get the police involved. See, Kevin's given the go ahead. He assures me it's all good, but I like to get it from the real boss's mouth."

She folded her arms across her chest. "If you think flattering me will get you anywhere, you're wrong." Talicia started to raise her hand to signal to the DJ.

"Your brother Tyjon. He's a nice guy…uh…girl. What does he prefer? Never mind. I know you want him safe, right?"

"You're threatening my brother?" The bottle shattered on the floor because she leaped at him and slammed him against the back mirror. More glass broke, and the rack holding a small collection of rare brands joined the rest of the mess. Talicia didn't care about any of it. "Do you know how many people I've met over the years who thought they could hurt Tyjon and get away with it?"

She threw a punch, and his head snapped around. Being white, his skin showed the mark right away, but his angry eyes blazed brighter rather than dulling from the impact of her hit. He wasn't much bigger than she was in build, but when his fist came up, Talicia quaked a little. He came straight for her nose but stopped on a dime and shoved her back. She fell around the side of the bar and landed on her ass.

Talicia's mouth hung open as he bent in front of her. "You think you're the only one who came up in the street?"

She couldn't find a response.

"We all did, and there's always someone more badass than you are. Now, let's have this conversation without the drama. If we do, you and your brother will come out better."

All he did was piss her off more, but she held it together. The DJ had probably called the cops with the glass breaking and them struggling behind the bar. She stood and brushed her hands off onto her pants legs. There would be a lot of cleanup to do before tomorrow night.

"Whatever. Say what you have to say, and get out. All I know is, whatever Kevin said you can forget it. I run this club, and he does nothing but collect."

The man grinned. "Funny. That's all I do usually. What's the smarter position to be in?"

She pressed her lips together.

He grew serious. "I want to do a little business through here. No one gets hurt. There won't be any violence. You look the other way. I give you a small cut. Not a big deal."

"No."

"Don't be stupid, Talicia."

"There's a million other clubs in New Orleans. Go find one of them. Not here."

He sighed. "Look, just like you said, there are a million other clubs. The competition is fierce. There's no real reason for any of your customers to come here over Joe Blow's place. I've had my eye on you a while. Your clientele is decreasing since that bigger club opened a couple miles from here."

"Go there then!" He was right, but she wouldn't admit it. The club was full on most nights but not as full as it used to be. Talicia made it her business to know what went on in New Orleans when it came to entertainment, and she had heard of the new spot before their grand opening.

Baldy's expression darkened. "I've already chosen the spot I want."

"And I've already decided you can kiss my ass. I run a clean club. No drugs. Don't look at me like that. It's obvious what you want to run through here."

He made another drink and drained the glass before setting it precisely on the counter. "Are you pretending to be clean, Talicia?"

"What's that supposed to mean?"

"Word is you'll do anything for your brother, that you've done any…*thing*."

Her blood ran cold, and a hundred thoughts vied for dominance in her head. "I don't know who you've been talking to, but they need to get their facts straight."

She wasn't sure what he referred to, the present, the past, both? Sure, she had done some things she wasn't proud of in the past. Some would call it major, some would dismiss it as nothing. Talicia liked the choice of keeping it where it belonged.

She speculated over whether he meant her "doing" Stefan, but that couldn't be it. Who the hell cared who she slept with? Plus her staff knew she had a white man sharing her bed. Most of them didn't give a crap. None as far as she knew associated Stefan the musician with Stefan Marquette the billionaire. However, that's where she worried. Was this piece of garbage in front of her threatening Stefan? If so, she would have to ask him never to come back. The prospect dimmed her world.

Aside from Stefan, he had threatened Tyjon, and that's where she drew the line. Tyjon couldn't defend himself. He never could. He'd been hurt too many times in the past until she grew strong enough to fight for him.

She was sick of it all, but it wasn't like she had to throw a punch now that they had grown up and were out of school.

Tyjon didn't know all she had done for him other than fighting, and Kevin met them when the battles were over. He knew nothing of her past, so he couldn't have run his mouth. So maybe this was all a bluff.

"Your life would get a lot less complicated if you cooperate. If you don't, well, I have to do what I have to do." He strode by her at his leisure. "Think about it."

Talicia watched him leave and then ran to lock the door behind him. She hurried up to the DJ booth and found Chez there shaking like a leaf. "Did you call the police?"

"No, I was scared to."

She frowned at him. "Chez, he could have killed me."

"I know. There are rumors on the street that he already has killed people. I hoped he'd never target this club because we're not big like a lot of the others, but I heard…."

He fell silent. She swiveled his chair around when he turned away. "You heard what, Chez? Spit it out."

"I heard he's looking to expand over this way."

"Who is he?"

"Marcus Colby. He's real bad news, Licia. Don't get mixed up with him. If he's picked out this club, try to change his mind because people end up disappearing. The police haven't been able to pin anything on him."

She swore. "This isn't some lame TV show. I'm not going in for all that mess. I just want to enjoy running the club. That's all."

He stood. "Yeah, well it don't always work that way. You want to do your thing, and other people want to take it or use you with it. That's how the world works."

Talicia ran a hand across her forehead. A sharp pain arrowed up her back and settled somewhere between her shoulder blades. She recognized it as stress but couldn't work it out no matter how hard she tried. Why couldn't people leave her and her brother alone? Why did they keep after them? All her life she had to fight. Why couldn't it be over, damn it?

If it was over, I guess I'd be dead.

No, she had to keep fighting and find a way to get out of this situation. She had always found a way in the past, and she would again. No matter what.

CHAPTER EIGHT

Two weeks later…

Stefan smiled and touched the back of one of his guests' chair as he leaned toward the group. "Hello, beautiful ladies. I hope your night is going well this evening."

The women tittered and squirmed in their seats, almost cooing at his attention. A strawberry blonde spoke up first. "We're great, Stefan, now that you and Damen are here, but we don't know what we want to order. Can you recommend anything?"

He touched his chest. "I'm flattered, and of course. My brother and I are here to serve you. We have the roasted chicken over Florentine rice, and of course, there's the duck. Let me assure you it is broiled to perfection. You will be satisfied."

Damen chimed in, oozing charm but not as flirtatious as he was before he met and married Heaven. If anything, Stefan noticed the women responded to him more. They adored the reserved aura of the nerd that was his middle brother. Stefan bet the women thought Damen was awkward and nervous around women. He knew better. Heaven was his heart and soul, and Damen would do nothing to betray her.

"I want the duck, Stefan," one of the ladies called out.

"The chicken, Damen," another responded.

Each seemed to find satisfaction in speaking their names. He and Damen didn't serve together normally, but this was a very large group, and they had reserved one of the upper dining rooms for their event. Stefan and Damen handled the initial greeting and order taking, and then another couple of servers would take over.

A little later on, Tiffany, one of the waitresses approached him, her face red with rage. "Stefan, that…that…"

"Guest," he supplied firmly but gently.

She grumbled, balling her fists at her sides. "Guest! That woman at table three is demanding you bring her food and not me. She says I'm too rude. Can you believe it?"

Several pairs of eyes swung Tiffany's way, all seeming to agree with what Stefan knew. Tiffany hung onto her job by a hair. Creed had come close to firing her on several occasions.

"Girl, please," Shada said, plating dirty rice with beef another customer had ordered. "You define rudeness. You should be glad you haven't been thrown out on your ass by now. Stefan's spoken up for you too many times."

Tiffany grumbled but ignored Shada's comment. "Stefan, it's against the rules for us to hand over our tables unless it's an emergency. Can't you tell her that?"

Stefan strode to the kitchen door and peered through the porthole window. "That's a congressman's wife, Tiff. We give them special treatment. I'll go."

She wailed.

"Oh shut up, stupid," Shada snapped. "If you're worried about Stefan taking your tip, ask him for it. Damn! And get out of my kitchen."

"It's not your kitchen," Tiffany shot back.

"Ladies." Stefan cast his voice low, but the emphasis sealed both of their lips. "Give me the order."

Tiffany gestured in silence to the tray waiting, and he hefted it into his arms, resting the back of the tray against his forearm. He didn't need a server to deliver the food as he could handle the weight.

Stefan reached the table and greeted the elderly woman with a smile. "Good evening, ma'am. I have your order right here."

"Oh, Stefan." She waved a hand at him. "Don't you ma'am, me. I'm not that old."

She was, but he didn't argue. He set a dish of fresh spinach with artichoke and cherry tomatoes in front of her and prepared to join it with the house soup when a freight train hit him. Stefan, because of his strength and size, managed to stay on his feet. However, the unexpected hit unsettled his tray and sent it flying. Glasses shattered on the floor, food stained the pristine white tablecloths. Guests cried out in alarm.

Stefan looked down at his chest to find the attacker wrapped around his middle sobbing and shaking. Fear crept up his spine, and he forgot about the guests as he tried to get Tyjon to let go so he could question him. This wasn't just dramatics, and he was sure of it.

"Ty, let go." Stefan tugged, but Tyjon's arms had locked on his waist. "What's going on? Why are you upset?"

"What's the meaning of this?" Creed's voice boomed. Damen snapped his fingers, and several waiters appeared to clean up the mess. As Damen apologized and soothed several guests, Creed reached a large hand toward the back of Tyjon's shirt. Stefan warded him off.

"I've got him. We'll go to my office." Stefan maneuvered Tyjon through the dining room toward the kitchen, and whispering broke out all around them. Anyone with eyes could see the smaller man, dressed in electric blue, was gay, and he clung to Stefan like a second skin. What they might not see was that Tyjon was still crying and shaking hard.

Duke held the kitchen door open for them, but his face was impassive. Jerome eyed him beside the door with a question in his gaze. Stefan sighed. "Stay close."

Jerome nodded and followed them into the kitchen, down the hall, and into his office. Stefan had scarcely gotten the door shut before Creed barreled in, followed by Damen. He realized he couldn't demand they leave so he moved Tyjon to the couch and forced him to sit down.

"Ty, what's going on? Why are you so upset?" He feared mentioning Talicia's name, but he strained to hear she was okay.

"Who is this man?" Creed demanded, "and why the hell is he disrupting Marquette's?"

Stefan didn't answer. He waited for Tyjon to suck in a breath. When Stefan's nerves were drawn to a breaking point, Tyjon spoke. "It's Licia."

Stefan surged to his feet. "What about her?"

"She's…" He started sobbing again.

Coldness clutched at Stefan's chest. He grabbed Tyjon by his arms and shook him so hard, his head flopped around. Damen was the one who pried him loose. "Let the man speak, Stefan."

"You'd better start talking now, Ty," Stefan threatened. He felt his brothers looking at him as if they didn't know who he was.

"I can't find her, and the club is a mess. Someone got in there and tore it up. There's blood and—"

Stefan broke for the door at a run. He heard his brothers asking what club Tyjon was talking about and what it had to do with Stefan, but he paid them no attention. Tyjon couldn't find Talicia? She never left her brother, *ever.* While they spoke of the trip together, she had been putting him off, telling him she wasn't sure about leaving at that time. He'd wondered if it had to with Tyjon, but now he wondered. Was it something else?

On the street, Stefan paced, waiting for Jerome to bring the car. He lost it and started to run around to the back parking lot, but Jerome screeched to stop in front of him. He jumped in and slammed the door. "Forget the lights, Jerome. I want to be there now!"

Jerome's hands gripped the steering wheel. "This sounds like a dangerous situation, Stefan, and we don't know all the facts. Let me drop you somewhere safe and assess it first."

Stefan eyed him. "You know my answer to that."

"If her brother doesn't know where she is, she might be in hiding."

"She wouldn't leave him, not voluntarily."

Jerome didn't argue, and Stefan knew he still didn't agreed with Stefan going to the club, but he didn't care. No one knew Talicia like he knew her. She wasn't as strong as she appeared. If she had a burden that had become too much for her to handle, *he* would find a way deal with it. Whether she liked it or not.

At the start of the narrow street where the club was located, police cars blocked access. Jerome stopped the car, and Stefan jumped out to head to the nearest officer. The man held up a hand. "Sorry, sir, this area's off limits for the time being."

Stefan strained to see past him. "Someone important to me owns a club right there, and I was told it was vandalized. I need to make sure she's okay."

"This is an active crime scene," the officer snapped. "No access, period. I don't care who you are."

Stefan felt agitated enough to consider ordering Jerome to go through this bastard, but he tried to think rationally. Even if they did get past him, there were a whole slew of other officers, who probably wouldn't think twice about shooting them down. He wouldn't do Talicia any good dead.

A small crowd of onlookers had gathered. Lights flashed from the police cars, and it seemed as if a million cars were in gridlock on the road. Two ambulances were parked near the entrance to the club, loading sheet-covered bodies, and Stefan's heart locked in his chest. He tried the officer again.

"At least tell me if you've found Talicia Clay. She's the owner of the club. Tell me she's not in one of those ambulances."

The officer remained stone-faced, and Stefan clenched his fist. A hand dropped onto his shoulder, and he was thrust aside. He looked over his shoulder to find Damen with his cell phone to his ear.

"Hey, chief, it's Damen Marquette. Listen, I have a favor to ask."

His brother chuckled at something the chief said. After a short exchange of words, he disconnected the call and folded his arms over his chest, looking smug. Stefan frowned at him, but before he could question his brother, another officer jogged over.

"Damen Marquette?" the officer asked.

"Yeah, that's me," Damen said.

"Let them through."

Damen's grin grew bigger, and he slapped Stefan on the back to propel him forward. Stefan dismissed his questions. All he cared about was that they were going to be allowed into the club. As soon as he hit the door, he had trouble drawing a breath. The damage was much worse than he had thought.

From the amount of glass on the floor, it seemed like every bottle of alcohol and the glasses were smashed. Chairs and tables were destroyed. The DJ booth's glass was cracked, and the security panel leading to Talicia's office hung on wires. Just as Tyjon said, blood mingled amid the glass shards, and someone's red handprint smeared the side of the bar. How could this have happened so quickly? He'd been here two weeks ago. Everything had been fine.

Crackling sounded behind him, and Stefan turned. Both his brothers entered the bar looking around. Their bodyguards were steps ahead of them, tense and ready for anything. Damen's astute gaze seemed to register every detail, but Creed's was filled with rage.

"Want to tell me what's going on, Stefan?" Creed asked.

"I guess I have no choice," Stefan said. "Somewhere amid this chaos, my wife disappeared."

"Wife!" Both his brothers shouted at the same time, and even Jerome appeared taken aback.

"Yes, Talicia is my wife. She's part owner of this club, and I need to find her."

"You're not just calling her that for the hell of it, are you?" Damen asked. "You married her?"

"Yes," he said again, without explanation.

"Are you out of your fucking mind?" Creed yelled. "You married someone you met in a club, *here?*"

"Creed, careful," Damen said.

"Bullshit, I'll be careful. He kept it a secret because he knew we wouldn't go for it. What were you thinking, Stefan? You wanted to be like us. You wanted a black woman because Damen and me have one? Fine, but you don't marry her!"

Stefan walked toward the stairs leading to the office. "For the record, I married Talicia long before Heaven appeared."

He didn't have to turn around to know both his brothers stood in shock. Instead, he started up the stairs, attention fully on what he would find when he reached the office. A shoe lay in the middle of the floor. The couch had been shredded with a knife, the equipment broken.

One of the desk drawers looked like it had been tampered with and abandoned. The drawer required just a little muscle to wrench it open. Stefan lost it when he found Talicia's purse inside, wallet and keys intact.

"Where is she?" he whispered.

"Call her," Damen said, walking into office.

Stefan slapped his forehead. He should have thought of that. Talicia kept her phone with her at all times. He speed-dialed her, but the call went to voicemail right away.

"What's her number?" Damen asked.

Stefan told him. He paced as Damen dialed a series of numbers on his own phone. While he listened, his gaze darted about the room. Stefan paced. He wanted to get out of there and check her apartment. He started to leave, but Jerome anticipated him.

"I got someone I trust to drive over to her apartment." He shook his head. "No one there. The good news is it doesn't look like it's been broken into."

Stefan roared. "Then I need to get out on the street! She could be anywhere."

Damen swung to face the officer that had followed them up. "Forensics been here yet?"

"No, sir," the young man who looked like a rookie said. "Not too long since it happened. The detective in charge is pissed the chief let you guys in. You're tramping all over the evidence."

"Don't worry. I got it." Damen tapped his head. Stefan recalled his brother had obtained a degree in forensics for no other reason than it seemed interesting at the time. He turned to Stefan. "Her phone is close. If she's with it, she hasn't left the building."

"We've searched the building," the officer said. "And the back alley. No one on the premises except us."

"I should be a cop." Damen smirked and stooped in the middle of the floor. He made a slow circuit on the balls of his feet. Stefan strained, willing Damen to figure out where Talicia was. If he was just showboating, he'd throttle him. He prayed Damen knew what he was doing. While his middle brother enjoyed joking around, Damen surely wouldn't choose now to do it with Stefan about to break.

"Damen," Stefan, growled. *"Please."*

"Easy, baby brother. Hang on a sec."

They all stood still, saying nothing. Stefan swayed on his feet, ready to shout for Damen to fucking hurry up. Talking that way to anyone, least of all his brothers, wasn't his way, but he felt like he was losing it. Each second might mean the last for Talicia if the blood downstairs was hers. Logic said it wasn't since the paramedics had carried out a couple victims already. His mental state didn't allow for clear thinking.

"Over here," Damen said at last. He moved to an

armchair that had been turned out of its usual position. They both studied the wall, and as far as Stefan saw, it looked normal. Damen crouched again and traced fingertips over the smooth surface. He impacted with the baseboard and shifted an inch or two to the right. Something creaked. The next thing Stefan knew, a child-sized panel opened in the wall.

"Holy hell," Creed whispered over Stefan's shoulder.

Stefan couldn't see far into the dark space, but he suspected something was in there. "Flashlight!"

The rookie officer appeared and shined a light into hole. At the other end, not moving, was Talicia. Stefan cried out and lunged for the hole, but he caught his wide shoulders on the wall and winced. He tried turning sideways but still no dice.

Damen grabbed his arm. "Let him try." He pointed a chin to the small officer, and the man set his flashlight down.

Stefan squeezed his arm in tight grip. "Be gentle with her. Slide her over here so I can get her. Watch her head."

"Let him work, Stefan," Creed ordered.

The officer dropped to all fours and crawled into the hole. Stefan realized the opening had been built for two people no bigger than Talicia and her brother. Somehow Talicia had been forced to go into it without Tyjon. He could only imagine the danger she'd been in to have made that decision.

He willed the officer to hurry, and soon the man's rear exited the hole as he moved backward in the confined space, dragging Talicia to the edge. When he was clear, Stefan shoved him aside to grasp her himself. He gave a sharp cry upon seeing her face. Blood caked in her short hair and smeared on her face. Her soft skin was bruised in several places, and both eyes were swollen shut.

No one made a sound as Stefan raised Talicia into his arms and carried her down the stairs. "The hospital," he said to Jerome when they reached the car. Stefan snuggled Talicia onto his lap and tight to his chest.

CHAPTER NINE

Talicia was getting out of the hospital. She had been there several days, and she couldn't wait to escape. What she wasn't looking forward to was the fact that Stefan refused to allow her to go back to her apartment. The only reason she agreed to go to his place was that he said Tyjon had been living with him ever since the incident. Her brother confirmed it the way he gushed about the luxury in which Stefan lived.

"Licia, you won't believe it, but he has a maid and everything. I haven't had to lift a finger. She even washed my drawers. Can you imagine?"

Talicia sighed. "You told me a hundred times, Ty. Don't overwork the woman. Just because she's a maid doesn't mean you can't do most things for yourself."

"Aw, you're being a spoilsport. I deserve this kind of treatment. As far as I'm concerned, I'm on vacation, and it feels great. You should relax too."

Talicia reached for the orange juice she hadn't drank earlier. Her stomach knotted. She'd already heard their secret was good and out. Tyjon had gushed like an idiot to find she'd married her billionaire and chided her for not telling him sooner. He was all smiles, but she saw the fear in his gaze that he tried to hide. Tyjon was scared, and he was the only reason she gave in to Stefan's taking charge.

As her fingers wrapped around the cup, her brother's overlapped hers, and he raised it with her to her mouth. She took a sip and pushed it away. "I'm fine. You don't need to act like I'm an invalid. Just a little bruised and swollen."

Her brother pouted, studying her face. "Let me put some makeup on you."

"No."

"Your eyes opened, but they look fat. I can do miracles with shadows."

"Buzz off, Ty. I don't care if I don't look like a beauty queen."

He squeezed her fingers, and she winced. Her knuckles were swollen. She'd thrown as many punches as she could. The problem was she was outnumbered and outclassed. In the end, she'd hidden. Knowing Tyjon was with his new lover was the single reason she went in, but she hadn't intended to stay in that hole. Then the pain was so much and the dizziness made it worse. She passed out. The next time she came to she heard Stefan's voice, so gentle but terrified for her.

"Ease up, Ty. We're okay, and when I get back on my feet—"

"You'll still live with me," Stefan interrupted as he strode in the door. Her heart skipped a few beats as she looked at him. Her hero, bigger than life, sexy, and he smelled good. The last part she got an up close and personal account of when he leaned in and kissed her.

Talicia turned her head too late. "Stefan, we're not going to depend on you. The minute I can, I'm putting my life back together. I did it once. I'll do it again."

"Too dangerous," he quipped and held out a bag to her. "Here. I bought you some clothes to change into."

When he said bought, she assumed he meant he stopped by her apartment and grabbed a few things. Instead, she opened the boutique bag to realize the items were actually from particular boutique named on the bag. Each piece wore a price tag, a hefty one.

"These aren't mine," she murmured going through them.

"They'll fit. Do you need me to help you get dressed?"

"No!"

He looked like he didn't get her protest given they were married and lovers.

"Get out, both of you." Talicia waited until both men had vacated her room, and then she took her time dressing. Just as Stefan said, the clothes fit. He'd either noticed her size in her old clothing or was a good judge. She had to admit she was grateful, especially given the clothes weren't overly girly and nothing like her brother would have worn. At the same time, she wished he had brought a dress. Maybe it would make her feel less like a beast. The bathroom mirror had shown the swelling had mostly gone down, but the bruises lingered. She looked awful, ugly to her own eyes, and she didn't doubt Stefan's family would show up at his house just to see the witch who must have tricked him into marrying her.

A short while later, Talicia climbed into Stefan's car. "Hey, Jerome. What's up?"

"Hello, Ms. Talicia. I'm glad to see you're doing okay."

"I'm all right. Thanks for coming to look for me with Stefan."

"Of course. That's my job."

She frowned. "I'm not your job."

He eyed her in the rearview mirror. "You're his wife."

She flushed and looked away. Guess he'd heard too. Who knew by his expression what he thought of her. Jerome had been with Stefan a long time, and they were somewhat like friends. She hoped he didn't think she was a gold digger, but she doubted he appreciated the danger she had brought to Stefan's doorstep.

At Stefan's house, Talicia gulped seeing that they had to pass through a security gate. She gaped at the manicured lawn and shaped bushes and noticed a couple men standing around.

Stefan drew her tighter to his side. Since they entered the car, he hadn't let her far from him. "They're extra guards. You don't have to worry about them. They're there to protect you."

"Stefan, you shouldn't go through all this trouble."

"Colby was released this morning. There's nothing to pin him to the attack on your club. I want to know you'll be safe."

She fisted her hands in her lap. "Those men were his. I know it, and the police have to know it. They even hinted around to it as soon as they started breaking up the place, telling me it was in retribution for getting him arrested. I wasn't going to let him run drugs through my club or threaten my brother and me. He wanted to get back at me. Now he goes free? It's not fair!"

Stefan covered her hand with a larger one of his. "I know, honey. Don't worry. I'll make sure he gets what he deserves."

She stared at him. "Don't get involved, Stefan, please. It would kill me if you get hurt."

"I won't."

"You don't know what you're dealing with. You've been sheltered."

"I wasn't always rich."

"But you didn't come from the hood, not like where I come from. It seems like every day I had to fight for Tyjon and me. And it was worse because he's gay."

He raised her chin and kissed her then leaned back to look into her face. "I'm glad you're willing to talk to me now."

She compressed her lips. "I'm not. I'm just tired."

"You'll sleep in today, and I'll stay with you."

"Don't you have to get to the restaurant?"

"I took off to pick you up from the hospital. Don't worry."

"Stefan—"

"Licia, please do as I say. For now. All I want is for you to recover and feel safe. Is that so hard? Would it hurt to make me feel better knowing you're not in any danger?"

She sighed and climbed out of the car as one of the men opened the door. Together, they walked into what looked like a mansion to her. The house probably was. Talicia had never lived in a house. All her life it had been apartments, even when her parents were alive. For a while, they moved from one to another. Yet, all of them were in that same crime-ridden side of town. Even the air over here seemed cleaner. She wouldn't let it go to her head. This arrangement was temporary.

"Which room am I staying in?" she said when they reached the second floor.

"Ours," Stefan informed her. "The master suite is this way."

She frowned at the back of his head as he led but didn't complain. Denying him at this point was useless.

She wouldn't get a lick of sleep being apart from him and knowing he slept in the same house. No sense fooling herself.

Stefan passed through double French doors onto the plushest carpet her feet had ever sunk into. She blinked at the massive bed and the heavy cherry wood furniture. This was luxury, and Stefan didn't seem to notice. The bedroom was so huge it could be sliced up into three rooms, and from the doorway to her left she looked in on another space that was big enough to be a bedroom. Living room furniture outfitted this one. Beyond that lay a ridiculously oversized bathroom with his and her sinks.

"Are you serious with all this?" she questioned him.

His eyebrows rose. "You don't like it? I suppose we could use one of the guest bedrooms."

"No, I mean… oh never mind. It's fine."

He strode over to her and caressed her arms. "Let me help you out of your clothes, and then I'll give you a bath and get you into bed."

Not a hint of desire showed in his expression. He was really worried about her health.

She wriggled away from his touch because bad thoughts did fill her mind, and every muscle already ached. "I can do it. Thanks."

"Licia, don't try to be strong on your own. I'm here for you."

"I know." She moved farther away and began unbuttoning her blouse. When his gaze locked on her chest, she turned from him. "Please, Stefan. I'm tired. I just want to be alone. I promise if I need anything I'll call you."

She lied because she wasn't going to call him or anyone else. Well, unless she collapsed on the floor, but her injuries weren't that severe. She had already gotten the report that Chez was dead along with one of the bouncers. A couple others were hurt, and no one had heard from Kevin. This whole mess was his fault, and when she found him, she'd make him wish he had left New Orleans and never come back.

The door shut silently behind her, and her shoulders slumped as she sat on the bed. She felt bad for lying to Stefan and pushing him away, but she meant what she told him. If he were caught up in the middle of this craziness, she didn't know what she would do. She loved him, but Stefan didn't seem to understand he was a musician billionaire who knew nothing of what she had to deal with growing up.

So what he used to be poor. That cutthroat look wasn't there, the hardness that came from clawing out of poverty and getting loose from the people who would hold a person down. All she saw when she looked into Stefan's eyes was sunshine. That was okay with her from the first time she met him because it warmed her. Not to mention the touch of his hands and his body.

She groaned, missing him, wishing she had taken him up on the offer to bathe her. He'd probably be good at spoiling her. "No, get a grip, Talicia. We're only here for a little while."

The insurance would kick in, she would get a big fat check, and she would redo the club. No problem. After that, she would convince Kevin to go away and leave them alone. Then she would hire better security. Maybe Jerome knew some people. She would have to sacrifice the extra money to pay them higher wages. No problem.

Talicia slept most of the afternoon and then spent the evening with her stomach in knots waiting for Stefan's family to show up. Not one of them stopped by. In fact, as the three of them—her, Stefan, and Tyjon—sat at the dinner table eating late because she had slept a long time, Stefan didn't even get a call or text.

She looked over at him as he sat at the head of the table being served by his maid. Jerome was nowhere in sight and neither were the other guards, but Stefan had told her all of them were around. She had never had so many people in the place where she lived.

"Can I have some more of that chicken too, Mary?" Tyjon gushed. "Everything is so good. I'm going to have to stay here forever."

The maid thanked Tyjon for his compliment and dished him more chicken. Talicia glared at him, but her brother was too busy smacking his lips and moaning. She rolled her eyes and turned to Stefan.

"Stefan, why haven't your family come? I expected them to grill me the second I woke up."

He looked at her in surprise. "No, I told them. No one disturbs you until we're ready. I threatened to block them if they even thought about it."

"You didn't."

He smiled. "Of course I did. You were very hurt. Both my brothers were there when we found you. In fact, if it wasn't for Damen, we might not have. I don't want to think about what would have happened if we hadn't."

"I'll have to thank your brother." She knew their names because of Tyjon's craze over celebrity types not because Stefan told her. Damen was one of them, but she couldn't remember which one. "Maybe we can stop by the restaurant before I go back home so I can tell him in person."

She didn't really want to go, but this seemed like a good opportunity to see Marquette's. With all Tyjon had told her he'd found online, she was curious. Then of course he had gone there to tell Stefan about her being hurt. She was grateful to her brother but kind of jealous too. He had seen Stefan's world first hand and probably met them all. That part she didn't look forward to. Still, thanking Damen was only right.

"Of course we'll go," Stefan said. "You'll be able spend time there as often as you want from now on."

"Stefan."

"This chicken is good, Ty. You should taste Mary's gumbo and cornbread."

Talicia wasn't fooled by Stefan talking to Tyjon about the food. He avoided her telling him again she wasn't staying long.

"Uh-uhn, boo boo," Tyjon protested. "I make some mean gumbo that nobody can beat. You try me see if I'm right. Will she get an attitude if I take over the kitchen sometimes?"

Talicia laughed. "I thought you were hooked on being served, Ty."

Her brother waved his fork at her. "I am, but Stefan threw out a challenge talking about Mary's gumbo. You know I make the best in New Orleans, Licia. Tell him."

"You do, Ty, but you don't have to prove it."

Her brother's lips poked out, and she cut her eyes to Stefan. Her husband grinned. "I guess we're in for Ty's gumbo tomorrow then. And in answer to your question, Ty, no Mary won't mind. This is your home now. You have free rein of the place. Both of you."

Tyjon whooped, and Talicia sighed. She didn't have the energy to fight Stefan on the matter. Then she figured it would make no difference one way or another. When she was ready, she would just go, and Stefan wasn't cruel enough to force her to stay. Some of the money she had saved in the bank would go to a lawyer who would draw up the papers, and she would be a single woman again.

Letting Stefan go was for the best anyway. This situation proved it. She'd held on too long, but it was really good while it lasted.

CHAPTER TEN

Talicia wandered over to the closet in Stefan's bedroom. He called the room both of theirs, but she still felt like this was his home. She had been there for a few days, and grew more comfortable. Too comfortable, she thought. In fact, it didn't even seem weird that the closet she entered was all hers and across from it was the one that belonged to Stefan.

On both sides of her were long spaces equipped with rings at the top for placing hangers, and at the bottom tons of shoe space. She had only a few of the rings occupied because it had taken her shouting at Stefan to get him to quit buying her clothes.

"Are you trying to say what I own isn't good enough?" she had yelled at him.

"Of course not. You always dressed well when I saw you at the club."

"Well, if you won't let me leave right now, then go get my clothes, and you can save your money!"

He'd fallen silent then, and she got worried. She kept prodding him, and in the end he'd admitted the truth. When they first checked her place, it was fine. Probably after Colby couldn't find her, he'd sent his men to trash the place looking for signs of where she'd gone. That news had shook her to her core because she really thought he would let it go after he destroyed the club. The man was crazier than she imagined.

"It was one arrest. Not like they convicted his ass," she grumbled, touching the dress Stefan bought. The piece was fancy if cut a bit deep in the front. A curvier woman would set off the folds better, but once again Stefan had gotten her size just right. He claimed he would take it back when she argued with him, but she'd hidden her joy at seeing it and said this was the last time. She could purchase her own clothes with her own money.

Talicia left the closet and returned to the bedroom to walk over to the dresser. She opened it to pull out a nightie she had ordered online. Up until now, she had worn T-shirts and men's boxers to bed. Stefan held her against his chest and not once did he try anything. She intended tonight to be different. Her aches and pains had lessened quite a bit.

Since she was getting to the point that she thought she could leave, she wanted to spend a few nights having sex with him. Who knew, she might be crying over Stefan for a long time, so she should have something to remember him by.

Talicia showered and pulled the nightie over her head. The silky folds fell to mid-thigh, and she looked at herself in the mirror. Lace and folds in the fabric at her breasts accentuated them and made them appear fuller. She rested hands on her hips and turned left and right.

Wait, what if Stefan hadn't tried anything because he lost interest? After all, there must be tons of thicker women with big boobs throwing themselves at him in the restaurant. Plus, he had started going back to work after two days of staying with her. He was there now and working late. She chewed her lip thinking about it. Maybe this was all for nothing.

Talicia turned her head to the side and touched a small area at her jawline that was still purple. The spot was tender where one of those goons had punched her. Tears welled in her eyes, but she blinked them away. She'd been punched before, grabbed, thrown down, stomped. That wasn't the first time, but she hoped with everything she had in her it would be the last.

I'm still a woman, damn it.

"Licia! You shouldn't be wearing that."

She jumped at Stefan's voice and looked toward the door. He'd moved so silently she hadn't heard him on the stairs. His words registered, and she hugged her middle. "Why not? What's the big deal? I don't deserve soft things?"

He didn't appear to have heard her. His gaze was locked on her body. A suspicion washed over her, and Talicia looked down. Yup, sure enough. Stefan's work pants were tented. He frowned and shoved at his cock as if it annoyed him.

"Honey, please go change. There's no way I'll be able to keep my hands off you. Just the material will give me ideas if it brushes my skin while we're in bed. I'll take a cold shower."

Talicia started laughing. "Are you serious?"

"Why wouldn't I be?"

She had to be sure she understood him. "You're *trying* not to touch me?"

"Of course. You've been hurt. Some spots are still bruised, and there's no way I'm going to make them worse by climbing on top of you. It's not right, but please don't make it harder by wearing that nightie."

"What if I just take it off?"

"Licia."

She drew the material up as if she would remove it but just let her pussy show. He looked stricken. Again his big hand tried to tame his dick, and she'd never felt so sexy. Talicia walked over to the bed and leaned back on it then raised one leg while running fingers along her slit.

"But I'm so hot tonight, Stefan. I can't help myself. You spoon me every time we're in bed, and I can feel your dick. All I want is to get it inside me."

"I never meant to tempt you."

"But I mean to tempt *you*." She smirked and turned over, pushing her ass in the air. Raising the nightie again, she looked back. Just as she hoped, the man was mesmerized. Oh, she was getting hers tonight all right. Let him deny her now. "You can take a cold shower, but I'm wearing this nightie to bed. Or I'm not wearing anything at all. It's your choice."

He tried again but his voice was so ragged, she knew he was gone. "I don't want to hurt you."

She lay atop the comforter. "I have a few spots that are sore. You can kiss them and make them better. Like right here."

Talicia raised her chin and ran fingers along her throat. She moved to her left breast. He choked. "Your breasts hurt?"

"My nipples are a little tight. Maybe if you suck them…"

"Hell," he muttered. In seconds his clothes were on the floor, and he climbed on the bed. He leaned down and kissed her belly while grasping her hip with a gentle touch. "You can lay on top of me. That way I won't make a mistake."

"You prefer the top."

"You said you're hot, right?" In one smooth motion, Stefan rolled over and pulled her on top of him. His thick shaft throbbed between them, and she rested her cheek against his chest and shut her eyes. For a few moments, Stefan didn't move even though she knew he struggled with his desire.

Talicia wanted to tell him she loved him and look into his eyes to see the same response. She might be bold and strong, but not that much, especially if what she saw there was revulsion. Love her? She was a whim, nothing more, and the whim would end at some point.

No, don't think about that. Think about how good it is to be in his arms now.

He always called what they did making love. That was his way. She called it sex, but in her heart, she made love to him with every caress and kiss. Talicia slid down his body, dropping kisses along the way.

"No, Licia. You can't," he protested.

"My mouth doesn't hurt," she lied. Her jaw was sore, but she intended to do enough licking to give him pleasure not take him too far into her mouth.

She licked the tip of his shaft and tasted precome. Parting her lips, she took the head a short way in and sucked, but Stefan jerked his cock away from her. She blinked up at him, surprised at the frown on his face.

"Don't lie to me," he snapped.

She gasped.

"You think I don't know every part of your body? I saw that bruise on your chin, and I know it was swollen not long ago. Come up here."

His anger threw her for a loop, and when she didn't move fast enough, he sat up and reached for her to slide her along his body to rest on his chest again. Stefan's huge hand covered the right side of her face, but the touch was light enough, it didn't hurt.

"Don't ever lie to me. I can't express how much I hate it."

"Stefan, I… I'm sorry."

He nuzzled her lips with his. She opened to him, and they tongue-kissed for long wonderful moments. When he broke it off, he whispered, "I can forgive anything."

"Except a lie?"

"No, I can forgive a lie, but I won't accept it. Please don't do it, Licia."

"Okay." She wasn't sure if she intended to keep her word or not. Up until now she just didn't share everything with Stefan. If she didn't choose to tell him a detail of her life, she just refused to talk about it. Lying wasn't an issue. What about later when she had to leave and if he asked her if she cared about him? No, he wouldn't ask that.

Stefan drew her legs apart and ran his hand over her ass. He slid her higher so he could reach her pussy and stroked fingers into the slick wetness. Talicia moaned and gripped his shoulders. She pressed her face into the pillow beside his head and shut her eyes. Stefan reached farther and brushed her clit. A quake rocked her body.

"We'll take it very slow and easy," he said.

"I can take it harder. Really, I'm not lying."

"I know, but we're taking it slow and easy."

He sounded like a broken record, but she got it loud and clear. Stefan was sweet until he was pushed too far. Then it was his way or his way. His alpha attitude kind of turned her on, and it wasn't like he didn't get her off with his fingers. Like he was doing right then.

Talicia cried out his name and arched her hips, pushing her ass up. Stefan's fingers sank all the way in her heat. He squeezed her ass cheeks and wiggled his fingers inside her. She thought she would pass out it felt so good.

"I want to pump so bad, Stefan."

He threw his arm around her middle to hold her still and began pumping his fingers in and out of her pussy faster. The stimulation had her moaning and panting, pleading for more. He took her to the point that her orgasm was about to crash down all around her. Then he pulled his fingers out and shoved his cock into her pussy instead. Talicia screamed his name through clenched teeth.

Stefan kept sharp control of her movements while grinding his dick into her heat. He arched his hips into the mattress and drove up. Again and again, he thrust, and all she could do was hang onto him, letting him give her pleasure.

"Stefan, let me go. I want to ride you."

"Not yet." He squeezed her ass and massaged it as he took her. The orgasm grew to fever pitch and then tore through her body. Talicia whimpered until it gentled, but Stefan continued to stroke into her pussy. When his hand on her back tensed, she knew he was ready to come. She clenched her internal muscles, squeezing his dick with everything she had. A sharp cry was all he uttered, and she felt his hot seed inside her.

Talicia panted as Stefan rubbed her back. He loosened his hold so she could get down. Instead, she stayed where she was, soaking up the feel of his hard body, his scent, the sound of his soft breathing, and the aftermath of him making love to her.

"Now you sleep," he said.

"We usually go all night."

"If you think I'm going to let you, you're wrong."

She grumbled, but she was worn out after one session. Maybe she should stay with him a little longer, until she was back up to snuff. Then they could have sex for hours. Yeah, then she could say good-bye.

CHAPTER ELEVEN

Talicia looked out the car window at the restaurant. Tall forest green letters spelled out the word Marquette's above the entrance. The glass doors sparkled in the sunshine as if someone had just that moment finished Windexing them. A couple in fancy clothes stood outside, the man checking his watch every so often. Were they that eager to get into the restaurant that they had arrived before it opened?

Jerome held the car door for her, but she didn't move. Her heart hammered in her throat. Stefan had said he would bring her today, but a situation at the restaurant had caused him to send the car and Jerome. He said he would be waiting, and she had hoped he meant on the curb. Now that she thought about it, she supposed he wouldn't wait on the curb. Not when his bodyguard attended to her. She'd have to make sure he didn't do that again.

"Ms. Talicia?" Jerome called when she didn't move.

She cleared her throat and climbed out. *Never let them see how scared you are.*

"They're good people," Jerome said as she passed

him. Talicia didn't respond but kept moving. At the door, she paused, and Jerome leaned around her and rapped heavy knuckles on the glass. Almost right away, the lock clicked, and the door swung outward. The man in dark slacks and white shirt with an apron about his waist didn't look anything like Stefan, so maybe he was just one of the waiters.

"Hello, I'm—"

The man nodded and backed up a little. "Mrs. Marquette. Come in."

She stiffened. "Talicia Clay."

The man's face reddened, but she moved into the cool interior of the restaurant. Her first impression was more luxury. This was like a five star restaurant with chandeliers and pristine tablecloths, shiny wooden floors and expensive artwork on the walls. Soothing music was pumped over the speaker system, a good one. Nothing canned and cheap for Marquette's.

Talicia stopped in the small lobby area directly off the large dining room. She glanced to her right and noticed a short hallway to another glass door. The sign on it also read Marquette's, but under the fancy font was the word bakery. Did they also own a bakery? Tyjon hadn't mentioned it.

"That's her?" someone said. "Looks just like the brother. I can't believe Stefan married that."

"Tiffany!" a woman barked with authority in her tone. "Go home for the day."

Talicia raised her chin and stiffened her spine. She strode farther into the dining room. Too bad she couldn't have worn the dress Stefan had purchased for her. The afternoon shift at the restaurant wasn't the right time for an evening outfit. She'd gone instead for simple gray slacks, but she had paired them with a soft pink blouse that she had liked on sight. If this was how they were going to judge her, well, it didn't matter anyway.

She walked over to the woman in the chef's outfit, who'd told the blond to go home. Was this the woman Stefan kept speaking about who taught him how to cook? She was pretty. Worse, she was hippy with unnecessarily big boobs. Then she turned, and Talicia realized she was pregnant. With whose baby? Talicia couldn't draw in a breath.

"I'm just starting my shift," Tiffany complained. "And you're not my boss anyway. Creed is."

The chef folded her arms over her chest. "Oh, you think you're staying here when I tell Creed I want you gone?"

The blond's mouth fell open. Then she snarled. "All of you think you're so special, taking our men. Now there's another one! You should stick to your own kind."

All eyes were on the young woman who must have lost her mind. Talicia wondered what kind of restaurant they ran here that the staff acted like this and mouthed off any way they liked.

The chef put her hand on her hips. "Oh, it's like that? Well how about this, Tiff? You can get your stuff and clean out your locker. You're fired."

"I don't care anyway. I was about to give my notice. I already found another job."

Several voices rose saying she was ungrateful of what the Marquette's had done for her. Some said she was just mad none of the brothers wanted her. No one seemed to support the woman in her outburst, but Talicia knew a few probably felt the same way. They just needed their jobs, unlike her.

Deep voices sounded nearby, and another door with a porthole in it opened. A huge man, slightly bigger than

Stefan, stepped through the door. His gaze first locked on the chef and lingered. She must be his woman, Talicia thought with relief. Then he looked at her and didn't say a word.

"What's all the shouting," the big man asked. "We're opening in less than half an hour."

"Creed, I fired Tiffany. I don't want her back here." The chef swung on her heel and marched across the room. The way she barreled down on Talicia, she wondered if she needed to raise her fists but thought better of it. The woman wasn't likely to throw any punches when she was pregnant—hopefully. "I'm Shada, Creed's fiancée. You must be Talicia."

"Nice to meet you." Talicia held out her hand to shake. She wished she could feel the greeting from Shada was friendly, but there hadn't been much emotion in the words, unless one wanted to call ice an emotion. In her head, she must be saying she wanted this other bitch to follow the first out the door and never see either again. Shada had the authority to fire Tiffany but not Talicia. "You can call me Licia if you want. Everyone does."

Shada eyed her up and down. "So what's your angle?"

Talicia didn't get to answer. The porthole door burst open again, and this time it was Stefan. He rushed over and moved around Shada in a flash to take Talicia's hand. "I'm sorry I was late. You're doing okay? Tired?"

Out of the corner of her eye, she saw Shada frown and look from Stefan to her and back again. She pulled her hand from his. "I'm fine, Stefan. Where's Damen? I want to thank him and get it over with."

"Oh, he only saved your life, and you want to get it over with?" Shada snapped.

"I didn't mean it like that," she growled back. "And he hardly saved my life when I was just bruised a little."

"Bruised? People died in that mess you dragged my brother-in-law into, bitch."

There was that bitch she was waiting for. Talicia stepped into Shada's face, but Stefan pulled her away and led her to the back of the restaurant. As they headed down a hallway, she tugged on his hold.

"Stefan, let go. I'm going to tell her about herself. I don't want her to think I'm scared of her. Apparently, she thinks she's the shit the way she told your brother she didn't want to see that woman anymore."

He said nothing but shuffled her through another door and shut it behind them. When they were inside he drew her close, but Talicia shoved his chest. He looked surprised at her rejection, and she compressed her lips.

"Licia, calm down. We knew this wouldn't be smooth, but I've been preparing them for—"

"Preparing them for what? Me?"

The door burst open, and the big man barged in. She recalled his name, Creed, the oldest one. So Damen was in the middle, and Stefan was the youngest. Behind Creed came two more men, the last two looking like twins with their similar sardonic smirks. The one twin wore glasses, but the other didn't.

"Is this an ambush?" she said, balling her fists and positioning herself for a strong stance. Inside, she wanted to throw up. This was too much like the club that night with Colby's men ready to beat her for daring to defy him. No violence he'd said. What a load of crock.

Stefan swung to face his brothers. "Whoa, we don't all need to be in here at the same time. You're scaring her."

"I'm not afraid of them!"

The one twin grinned. "She doesn't look scared, Stefan. I admit I'm surprised though. I thought it was the other one."

Talicia glared. "Who are you?"

He shouldered through the group of big men and stuck his hand out grinning. "I'm Duke Marquette. You must be Talicia Marquette, Stefan's wife."

She had the feeling he got pleasure from rubbing her existence in to the others and resented him for using her for entertainment. He might smile, but he didn't care about her any more than Shada did. What did he mean he thought it was the other one, what other one? Another woman?

"My last name is Clay not Marquette," she said. "I thought there were only three brothers."

"Clay," Duke said. "That's interesting. I'm the cousin."

"Leave her alone, Duke." Another man stepped up, the one with the glasses. "I'm Damen."

"Oh." She accepted his hand and smiled this time. "Thank you for helping Stefan to find me. I could have handled it eventually, but I'm sure he was worried. So thanks."

"My pleasure." Damen smiled, and it looked genuine. He might just be a different kind of charmer or it was an illusion of his glasses. She reserved judgment. He didn't even try to pretend he wasn't studying her. "So you're really my baby bro's wife? You said your last name is Clay?"

Her gaze slid from him to the biggest man who still hadn't walked over. He radiated anger, but he never stopped staring at her. She resisted shifting under the accusation plain in his expression and tried to stand taller. That was hard to do when all four of them towered over her and made her feel like a dwarf. No, a troll, an ugly one because these men were the beautiful people. All four of them could have any woman they wanted, multiple women who were willing to share if they could get one night.

Talicia fell to her old standby, the tough shell she had been using all of her life to survive. "Yes, if you're wondering if the marriage is real or fake, I don't care. Look me up. Check into my background. I can tell you the gist right now. Poor, black, and from the wrong side of town. High school education."

"I bet there's more to you than that," Creed said, coming forward.

"And I'm sure you already know," she shot back.

"Of course." He bared even white teeth, but it wasn't a smile. "You married my baby brother, who I would kill for to protect him. I'm going to dig up every kernel of information I can about you. So if there's anything you want to reveal, do it now. Although, the incident that got you hurt is bad enough. If my brother had been there at the time…"

He left the rest unsaid, and Talicia felt the same threat she'd felt from Colby's men.

"Creed." Stefan shoved Talicia behind him. "We talked about this. I told you I wouldn't let her come if you were going to threaten her. I mean it. She's my wife, and she won't be disrespected!"

"Baby *bro* has balls," Duke teased. "A woman will do that to you."

"Shut up, Duke," Damen growled. The way he said it made Talicia wonder if Damen didn't like Duke. If Damen didn't like him, the most decent of Stefan's family so far, her view of the man wasn't much better. He was an asshole and seemed like the type to start trouble. She'd hired a couple people like him before, but they didn't last long. Talicia didn't stand for it, but family was a different matter. Well, he wasn't *her* family.

"I'm making my position clear," Creed said. "We've dealt with this kind—"

"This kind!" Talicia moved around Creed. "Who the hell do you think you are calling me a kind? You don't know me, and don't think I'm going to cower because you threatened me either. So what you're big. I've taken down men like you and barely broke a sweat."

"Whoa," Duke crowed, grinning.

Talicia went on, ignoring Duke. "You don't scare me, and like I said I don't give a fuck what you think—any of you. I'm leaving, Stefan. I don't need Jerome to take me. I can find my own way."

She started for the door, but Creed grabbed her arm. "Hold it."

Talicia didn't think twice. She assumed he was about to attack her, so she let him have it as hard as she could. Jarring pain raced through her fist and up her arm. Nausea rolled through her system, but she kept swallowing to keep her breakfast down.

Creed's head went back, and then his big body followed. He staggered and smashed into a table holding a printer. The printer hit the floor with a crash, and the stack of papers that had been atop it flew everywhere. No one in the room said a word, but she felt every one of their eyes on her.

Talicia kept her fists up, one foot just ahead of the other. Before the attack, the hit wouldn't have fazed her, but she swayed a little, and her vision blurred. She wasn't all the way back one hundred percent. That and the fear of meeting them all threw her off her game.

Creed caught himself and worked his jaw, rubbing it. If he was angry before, he was liable to catch fire now. He looked at her and then to Stefan. "You married her,

Stefan?"

Talicia glanced at Stefan, who hadn't said anything or moved since she attacked his brother. He wore a stricken expression, eyes wide, jaw slack. Then it switched to sharp disappointment, and her stomach dropped. Damn, why couldn't she control herself?

"She's violent, unladylike, dangerous…" Creed ticked them off on his fingers.

"Creed," Stefan began, and Talicia couldn't believe the conciliatory tone in his voice.

She swung on her heel and wrenched the door open. In the hall, two women were rushing toward them, one being Shada. The other woman, also black did a double-take on seeing Talicia. She had a softness to her and was of course pretty. Behind the woman a boy and a girl followed, eager and nosy expressions on their faces. Talicia moved around all of them to keep going.

"Hold up," Shada demanded. "What's going on back here, and where are the guys? We're about to serve the guests."

Talicia swore. "I killed them all in that office on the right."

The softer woman made a small sound of alarm. Shada glared. "You're so not funny. See what I told you, Heaven? Don't worry. Her small ass can't do anything."

Talicia stopped walking and swung back to face them. They'd halted when she passed by. She strode up to Shada with her hands on her hips. Both of them had Talicia by an inch or two. Shada looked like she could do some damage, but the other woman probably hadn't hit anyone in her entire life.

"When you see your man, don't think he's too much of a punk. They bruise so easily."

Both women's eyes rounded. Shada choked over her

words, trying to speak. The boy moved up to Talicia looking at her as if she were a museum exhibit. "Whoa, you hit Uncle Creed? That's crazy brave."

Heaven yanked the boy back toward her. Shada got a hold of herself and pushed Talicia's shoulder. "You put your hands on Creed? First thing here, you attack him after they all went out to try to save your sorry ass?"

"Just like I told him, you don't know me. You need to back up."

"Or what?" Shada demanded. "You'll hit me this time?"

"Fuck off."

"She's got a mouth on her, Heaven."

"So do you, Aunt Shada," the girl said.

"Nita, shut your lips," Heaven whispered. "I told you two not to follow us back here. Gideon, go get Weaver."

Up until then the men's voices had been somewhat raised behind the closed door of the office, but it opened just as the little boy returned with this small built white man who had the look of someone dangerous. Talicia swung her head back and forth in both directions. Creed led the brothers, and behind this Weaver guy were two other gigantic men.

"So all of you are coming against me?" Her fingers throbbed, and her arm muscles were sore, but she raised her hands, putting the wall at her back.

"Move," a deep voice bellowed, and then Stefan was coming at her. She tightened her mouth to keep her lips from trembling and narrowed her eyes. He laid gentle hands on Shada and Heaven to shuffle them aside and propelled the kids out of the way by the tops of their heads. They bobbled aside like baby ducks, and then he stood in front of her. "Licia, you don't have to fight anymore."

He knew from grabbing her at her apartment what she'd do, but he wrapped his arms around her anyway. From the look of it, he didn't even hesitate to drag her into his embrace. She couldn't see past his shoulder, but she heard the gasps all around.

"Oh, Stefan," Shada said, "you're so innocent."

"Let it go, Shada," Heaven whispered. "It's his decision."

"Like hell I will. Wait, Creed, are you okay? The bitch said she hit you."

Talicia struggled in Stefan's hold, but he drew her closer to his chest. She was no match for his strength. Stefan's lips touched her ear. "Calm down. I'll take you home."

"You have to work." Her words were muffled, but he seemed to hear.

"You are more important."

Because she didn't have the energy to fight him and she didn't want the others to see her weak, Talicia let Stefan walk her out into the main dining room. Guests were starting to arrive, and waiters seated them. Several women greeted Stefan as they passed, and he nodded and smiled to them. Eyes full of jealousy flicked to her, and she imagined they questioned who she was since Stefan kept his hand pressed against her lower back.

At the front, Jerome opened the door. He hadn't crowded into the hall with others. She didn't know if it was because he already knew she didn't pose a threat or that he hoped the others would kill her and be done with it. Why she was thinking of this family of restaurateurs as mobsters, she didn't know. Then again, Creed did threaten her life. Who knew what they were into.

Jerome opened the car door, and Stefan ushered her inside. Talicia sat with her arms wrapped around herself, but when Stefan settled beside her, he took her left hand in his. He examined her knuckles, brushing a finger over the ridges. "They're swelling. Licia, why did you do that?"

She jerked away. "I'm sorry I hurt your brother. No, actually I'm not."

"I hoped for a better meeting."

"Well then, I'm sorry I embarrassed you."

He captured her chin, but she pulled away. "You didn't embarrass me. I know you're always scared that—"

"I'm not scared, Stefan! He threatened me. What was I supposed to do?"

He didn't say anything for a few minutes, and she slid away from him. Having her thigh touch his bothered her. Stefan touching her in any way made her forget he was one of them too, even if she was married to him.

"You were supposed to let me handle him," he said in a low tone.

"I don't need you to fight my battles. Besides, it looked like Creed doesn't respect that you're your own man. He thinks you're his baby brother who he has to bully small women for."

Stefan chuckled. "It seemed that way."

She glared at him and then smirked. "My guess is he's been looking out for you all your life and thinks you can't make your own decisions."

"Sounds familiar."

"What's that supposed to mean?"

"Nothing. I'm going to talk to him. I won't let him treat you the way he did, but I also don't want you fighting. Do we have a deal?"

"No."

"Licia."

She sighed. "I hate them. They hate me. I might as well stay away. Everyone would be happier."

He folded his arms over his chest and leaned back in the seat. "So you're going to let them run you off?"

Talicia froze. "Excuse me?"

He shrugged. "You're my wife."

"For now," she insisted.

"Okay, for now. You're my genuine wife. You didn't coerce me into marrying you, and you've never taken anything from me in almost a year of us being married. You have just as much right, *more* right than Shada to the name and the Marquette's holdings. Yet, you'll let them make you feel like you don't belong? Is that fine with you, honey?"

She bristled. "I don't have to prove myself, Stefan."

"No, you don't."

Still, he had her thinking. Shada had acted like the big woman in charge, bossing everybody around, including Creed. Meanwhile, Talicia had run off. If she didn't come back, Shada would think she won, and Creed would feel like his threat put her in her place. *Oh hell no!*

Even if it killed her and she hated every minute of it, she would be back. Let them all kiss her ass if they didn't like her. For the time being, she was also one of the family.

CHAPTER TWELVE

"Stefan," Talicia called as she slid to the end of their bed and dropped to her feet. He didn't answer, so she walked through the sitting room and farther to the bathroom. The evidence of him having taken a shower was there, but no Stefan. She returned to the bedroom and wrapped a satin robe around her, belted it at the waist, and padded barefoot to the hall.

On the upper landing, she leaned on the railing to listen. Deep voices sounded below, and she moved toward the stairs. At the foot of them, Jerome stood adding information to his cell phone. She scarcely set foot on the first step before he turned around.

"Ms. Talicia, everything okay?"

"Yeah, I was looking for Stefan."

"He's in the kitchen. We're about to head over to Marquette's."

Of course. After that argument at the restaurant, she'd gotten sick, throwing up, weak and shaking. The fact pissed her off, but there wasn't anything she could do about it. At least the effects had lasted just two days, and she woke up late that morning feeling a whole lot better.

Stefan insisted she sleep in longer. She had. Now, she wanted to tell him her idea. She was glad she had caught him before he left for the restaurant after coming home to check on her.

In the kitchen, she realized his voice had been so loud because he was on the phone. Her stomach knotted hearing Creed on the other end. Then Talicia dismissed the asshole from her thoughts as she watched Stefan ladling thick liquid into a bowl and setting it on a tray. Mary stood nearby wringing her hands like she wished he would get out of her kitchen and let her handle things.

Talicia went all warm and fuzzy inside. During the times Stefan brought a tray to her while she lay in bed, he must have been preparing the meal himself. He was so damn sweet. How she loved him.

"I'm up and feeling better," she announced from the doorway. "You don't have to feed me, Stefan."

He glanced up and smiled, the warmth in his gaze stealing her breath away. "Creed, I'll talk to you when I get there."

Stefan waited for his brother to agree and then punched the button to disconnect the call. He went on smearing jam on a thick slice of homemade bread and set the saucer beside the bowl of soup. She was so over soup, but it was the only thing she'd been able to hold down the last couple of days.

"You shouldn't be out of bed," Stefan said.

"I'm better. You saw for yourself this morning, and you pushed to get me to rest longer. Well, I did. Now I'm up, and I'm staying up, mister. So don't even try it."

"I could carry you there."

Mary's cheeks pinked, and Talicia laughed. "No, thank you. Plus, I'm done with the soup. It's good, Mary, but I want meat."

"Talicia," Stefan began.

"Stefan, I want to go to Marquette's. I've got an idea you might agree with."

"Can we discuss it upstairs?"

She tightened the belt on her robe. "No. You fired that one girl, right? If you haven't hired anyone new yet, let me fill in. I used to work as a waitress years ago when I first started out."

His eyes widened. "That's going backward for you."

"It wasn't going backward for you. And it's not forever. The insurance company said it could take up to three months for the investigation to be completed. I say that's bullcrap, but whatever. I can't force them to give us the money for the club now. All I can do is work. You can pay me too because I'm not working for free."

He chuckled. "All I have is yours."

"Don't talk like that around your family. Will you consider it?"

"Creed does the hiring, but I like the idea. I'll put in a good word for you."

She raised an eyebrow at him. "I want to go with you now. Jerome says you two are about to head back."

"Licia, you just told me this idea." He picked up the tray and started out the kitchen. The stubborn man was going to take it upstairs anyway. She followed him.

"What happened to all that talk about me staying and showing them who I am?"

"You are staying."

"Yeah, but hiding out at your house isn't showing anyone anything. Are you ashamed of me or scared I'll beat up your brother?"

"Neither."

She thought she heard a snort behind her as they headed up the stairs. Talicia focused on Stefan's ass and resisted smacking it. She already knew how great it was for hanging onto while he jammed her pussy full of his cock. Just thinking about it made her want it, but she kept her mind on the task at hand.

"Then why won't you let me go?"

"I'm not stopping you from coming to the restaurant, Licia. I just don't want you to think you have to work. You were barely out of the hospital before you got sick. I feel like this is our fault for putting too much stress on you. It might be too soon to work. Marquette's can get hectic."

"You're being overprotective. I worked six days a week from the time I woke up until after four in the morning. I'm not a stranger to work."

They arrived in their bedroom, and Stefan set down the tray. "Eat, please."

She didn't move. "If you don't take me, I'm calling a cab or a taking a bus. If you don't talk to Creed for me, I'm going to ask him for a job myself. So you can let me suffer the humiliation when he turns me down just to get back at me."

Stefan frowned. "I won't let him get away with that!"

She grinned. "Good, so I'm going to shower and get dressed. Wait for me."

He sighed. "Fine. Eat first."

Talicia gave in to the meal, vowing to grab a cheeseburger from somewhere later. She rushed to get ready so not to keep the two men waiting, and soon they arrived at Marquette's. Her stomach tumbled all over the place, but she told herself no matter what anyone said, she wouldn't swing on them. If she was going to change their minds about her, then she had to act like a professional.

Talicia stood in the lobby while Stefan walked back to

talk to Creed. She took her time moving farther into the restaurant, rubbing her arms while she looked around. They arrived in the thick of things when guests were constantly coming and going. Waitresses and waiters zipped about, taking orders and refilling drinks.

A low buzz rose above the crowd, and over it the music played. Talicia scanned the dining room to spot a man playing a baby grand. His fingers tickled the ivories with skill, and while she didn't have any knowledge of music other than what she did and didn't like, she imagined he couldn't touch Stefan's ability.

Across the room, she spotted an arm waving and a big grin and rolled her eyes. What the heck was Tyjon doing here? Then she figured he was probably taking advantage of being an in-law. Great. She was trying not to look like she was using Stefan for his money, but her brother ate at the restaurant probably every chance he got. She knew without a doubt Stefan would have made sure he never paid.

"Hey, beautiful." Duke whisked by with a wink and a smile, but he kept moving as he led someone to their table. She was glad he kept going.

The kitchen door opened, and Creed appeared. All of a sudden, she felt like she was having the relapse Stefan was so worried about. *Get it together, Licia.*

He arrived in front of her. "I hear you'd like a job. I can let you start on a trial run right now if you think you can handle it."

Talicia looked pointedly at the bruise on his chin, and he reddened. "Just give me an apron."

He eyed her up and down. She'd forgotten she had hoped to work tonight. If she was honest, she'd admit she chose the skirt because it looked more feminine than what she had worn the last time. He'd called her unladylike, and she didn't usually rise to people's ugly opinions. However, her feelings were most hurt because of how she felt about herself and because it was Stefan's family.

"There's probably a uniform or two in the back," he said. Karey will show you." Creed gestured to one of the waitresses, and Talicia watched in amazement as a waiter saw Creed's signal and relieved Karey of the plate she carried all in a heartbeat. They exchanged a few brief words, and the guy was off while Karey approached Talicia and Creed. Damn, he drove a precise ship.

By the time Creed turned from Karey to her, Talicia had schooled her features. He didn't need to know she admired his work. Her intent was to impress him with the fact that she wasn't a wild animal.

"So you're Stefan's wife," Karey said when they were in the locker room. "I can't believe it. No one knew he was married."

Talicia stiffened, but the woman turned away and opened a cabinet. She dug through several pairs of black pants and white shirts. They appeared brand new. After a few minutes, Karey pulled out two pairs of pants and handed them to Talicia. Her smile never wavered.

"It's good to meet you, Mrs. Marquette. Is it okay if I call you Talicia?"

Talicia blinked. "Um, you can call me Licia if you want."

"Great, and you can call me Karey or Kare. I wasn't sure of your size, but these two are the smallest we have. You don't have to worry about them being gross or anything. They're practically new because the temp girl who wore them was terrible, and she was let go after like an hour. What a nightmare. Plus, they've been washed."

Talicia laughed. "So it gets pretty lively around here?"

"Oh yeah. You came at the right time. Tonight, Stefan is supposed to sing, but you've heard him sing before. He's so dreamy. All the ladies—uh—"

"It's fine, Karey. I know, and yes, I've heard him sing. He's something special."

"That's why you married him, right?" She smacked Talicia's arm in her excitement, and then left to give her time to change. Talicia chose the smallest of the pairs of pants to pull on and sighed. They were a couple sizes too big and were baggy on her. The smallest shirt hung like drapes. She did the best she could, tucking it all in and belting the pants with the belt she'd worn with her skirt.

When she straightened her arms, the sleeves fell a couple inches past her fingertips. She rolled them up and tied on an apron. Well, here went nothing. Either the animosity would end tonight, or they would all have a stalemate and it would take some time. Either way, no one would look down on her at the end of the shift. She would serve the hell out of those customers and leave them all smiling and happy.

"Okay, Licia, your tables are right here, three and four. You'll take the order and let the servers deliver the food," Karey explained. "No need to seat anyone. The hosts will take care of that."

Talicia frowned, looking where Karey indicated. "Three and four? Just two tables? Surely, each person is responsible for more than that."

Karey held up her hands. "Sorry, I have my instructions. I give you two tables and that's all."

"Who gave that order?"

"That's what Creed said."

Talicia clenched her hands at her sides. Did he trust her so little he didn't want to risk her screwing up too many orders? The way he spoke to her, she would have thought he'd get off on making sure she was overwhelmed and therefore messed up. When she turned in the direction of the kitchen, she spotted Stefan. Then she knew the truth. That bum had convinced Creed not to let her take on too much. Jeez, he acted like she was made of freaking glass.

Talicia had spent the time she and Stefan were married away from him. Now, she was starting to get to know more about the man he was. Well, he could forget about her falling into line with his plans, that's for sure.

"Don't worry about me, Karey," she said. Talicia whipped the floor plan out of the woman's hands and studied it. "I'm assuming you're responsible for this area from here to here, filling in for the missing girl?"

"I am, but another temp is coming in a little bit. Turnover in this business is outrageous."

"I know." Talicia handed the sheet back. "I'm taking over five and six along with the ones you gave me already until she gets here. You can argue about it, but I need to take orders. Those folks look hungry."

Talicia left Karey standing there with her mouth hanging open. She was lucky there was a gap in the help she could fill in, and arriving guests kept Karey from tattling on her right away.

"Good evening, everyone." Talicia smiled at the guests at table seven. "I'm Licia, and I'll be happy to be your server. How is everyone doing tonight?"

The chorus of voices washed over her, and she took down their requests. There were a few moments of awkwardness because she had no idea of the menu other than the specials for the evening.

Talicia paused, pen poised above her notepad. "You know what, I'm not sure about that, but I'm going to check immediately for you. We can figure something out."

She was about to turn when a hand touched her lower back. Craning her neck, she looked up into the gentle eyes of her husband. "Can I help?"

Talicia's heart banged against her ribs. The women around her tittered and greeted him by name. She wasn't surprised, nor did it rile her. Stefan had the answers she sought, but he wasn't wearing an apron. After they were done, he followed her as they left the table.

"You're handling four tables, Licia?"

"And I'm doing a bang-up job too."

One side of his mouth turned up. "You're so modest."

"Of course. Anyway, you're not serving? I thought you waited tables like Damen."

"I do, but not tonight. I'm singing. Will you come up and let me serenade you?"

"Heck no."

He looked disappointed, and she left him standing there to return to work. All the same, her attention kept straying to where he was, and she knew the moment he took over the piano from the man who had been performing up until then.

A different hum rippled through the crowd as soon Stefan sat down. She peered around at the rapt faces, and pride rose inside for her husband. Stefan was a born entertainer, and no one was immune to him when he played.

The kitchen door swung wide and fast, and the boy she had spotted the other day came rushing into the dining room. His gaze locked on Stefan, and then he scanned the room. When he spotted her, he hurried toward her. What was that about? The door opened again, and at a more leisurely pace, the young girl strolled over.

"Hey, Aunt Licia," the boy said. "Do you know me? I'm Gideon. We saw you the other day after you fought—"

She covered his mouth, rolling her eyes. "Yes, Gideon. I remember. I assume you've been told about me. You don't have to call me Aunt Licia."

"If I don't show respect, Mom will lecture me."

"Oh, well whatever then."

The girl drew up beside them. She said nothing, but at least she didn't cast Talicia any evil glares. The three of them looked back at Stefan as he began to sing. For a while, Talicia was caught up listening to him. When she thought she might be too obvious, she forced herself to look away. That's when she caught the rapt expression on Gideon's face.

"He messed up right there," the boy muttered. "Lower. It would have been better in a lower key."

She blinked at him. Who were these people?

"This next song," Stefan announced into the microphone, "goes out to a very special person. She knows who she is."

Talicia stiffened, but Stefan's gaze swept the crowd in such a way, any woman present might think the song was for her. Well, any who didn't have sense enough to realize it was an entertainer's way.

When Stefan began crooning words that spoke to her heart, however, her throat closed. "I know sometimes you're afraid and you pretend it's not true. You're so strong and so fragile at the same time, but I'm here. Look at me. I'm here."

She sucked in a breath and spun on her heel to hurtle toward the exit. All she could think about was getting outside to the fresh air. Unfortunately, the humidity of the night hit her hard in the face as soon as she opened the front door. She kept moving and shoved the door shut. Stefan's voice snuffed out, and Talicia managed to calm down a little.

"He wasn't singing to me," she whispered. Stefan composed music all the time. That was his nature, and he wouldn't be any good if he didn't write lyrics that spoke to the heart. Still, she found herself blinking, trying to keep the tears in check. Why the hell was she getting so weepy lately?

She moved a little way down the walk to the end of the building and leaned on the wall. Shutting her eyes, she concentrated on evening out here breaths. If she didn't get back in there, Creed would say she shirked her responsibilities, and he would have an excuse to fire her. Then the work she had done over the last few hours would be for nothing.

Talicia shook herself and turned to head back inside, but a man, who appeared out of nowhere blocked her path.

CHAPTER THIRTEEN

"Hey, baby girl, want to have some fun?" The man blew a ball of hot, stinky breath in her face.

Talicia recoiled. She was about to shove him away because he was standing too close, and it looked like he was about to topple over onto her. A hand snaked out from behind the man and landed on his shoulder. "Careful, pal. You don't want to fall."

Of all the people who could have come out it had to be Duke. She started around the man, but he didn't want to give up on her. He reached out to grab her arm, but Duke stepped forward, smiling at her.

"Licia, we should get to know each other better," Duke said, flirty as he moved closer to her. Somehow his elbow caught with the man's stomach. Talicia frowned. The impact seemed accidental, even casual. Yet, the drunkard doubled over, crying out in pain. For just an instant, Talicia thought he raised angry, hateful eyes to Duke. Then they went dull again, and he whined about rough characters on the street. Duke slapped him on the back. "Oh, I'm sorry, pal. So clumsy. Guess it comes from working too hard. Listen, let me buy you a cheeseburger."

"Duke." Talicia pulled at his arm, but it was like steel. "You're squeezing his neck too hard."

"No, he's fine. So how about that cheeseburger?"

The man managed to shake off Duke's hold and semi-straightened. "No way. I don't like the food at Marquette's. Too expensive and too fancy."

With that the guy wandered off down the street, wobbling side to side as he went. Talicia stared after him shaking her head. Duke stood in silence beside her, and she felt his gaze on her face, but she ignored him. When she started to go inside, his voice stopped her.

"We're right in front of the restaurant, but you shouldn't venture outside alone."

His tone was deadly serious, and when she glanced at him, his eyes were hard. She swallowed. This was the smartass she'd met, and she realized there was a lot more to him than she first believed.

"He was drunk, but I could have handled him."

Duke's slow grin resurfaced, and his eyes softened. "Yeah, I bet you could. After you slugged my cousin, I have a whole new respect for you."

"Is anyone going to let me live that down?"

"You're famous."

She swore.

"And such a potty mouth. What a combo with my sweet cousin Stefan, who wouldn't dream of cursing in front of a lady. I would love to hear the story of how you two met. Let me take you out."

"No, thank you." She headed back to the door but called over her shoulder. "And don't think you can charm me into anything with you either."

"Because I don't have any money?"

She stopped again and whirled around. "Excuse me?"

"Down girl. I don't care to experience that left hook."

Talicia glowered at him. "I doubt I could get a hit on you. The elbow to the stomach back there. That wasn't an accident. You meant to hurt that man."

"Are you calling me a bully?"

"I've known a few."

"Were you bullied, Licia?"

She rolled her eyes. "I'm also not having a heart to heart with you. I don't know what your game is, but I'm not buying, Duke. Please bother someone else."

"You break my heart, Licia."

"Stop saying my name so much!" He was really pissing her off. Nothing she said got to him.

He threw his head back and burst out laughing. Talicia's fingers itched to wipe the smile off his face but no more fighting Stefan's family under any circumstances. She had made the vow to herself, and she would keep it.

After an eternity, Duke pulled himself together. "I like you. You have fire. For what it's worth—and I'm guessing very little—I can tell you're not a gold digger."

"You're right. It's worth less than zero." She lied. Duke didn't hate her, and it seemed like the kids didn't either. This was progress. Sure, it shouldn't matter because when the dust settled and she got her insurance money, she would be gone. Despite that, she couldn't suppress the hope that her connection with Stefan would continue. Wanting them all to at the least accept her wouldn't die either. "I have to get inside. I've been out here long enough, and Creed will think I ran off."

"Ah, impressing the big dog. If you like, I can tell you how to do it."

Talicia jerked the door open and walked inside. As soon as she passed the threshold with Duke crowding too close behind her, she spotted Creed heading their way.

Her stomach curled up into a ball. She swallowed and took another step in his direction, but Duke shouldered past and blocked her view.

"Cousin, I have to talk to you about something," Duke said, an urgent tone in his voice.

Talicia stopped walking. She willed herself to move around Duke and face the music, but she couldn't raise her foot. Waiting for Creed to respond to Duke took years off her life for some ridiculous reason. She shouldn't care what he thought or did.

"You're in as much trouble as she is," Creed said at last. "I told you no shirking your job, Duke. You wanted to stay at Marquette's, and I gave you the chance."

This news surprised her. So Duke wasn't as tightly in the fold as the brothers. Then again, why would he? She recalled what he had said, that he didn't have any money. She didn't know his circumstances since she wasn't up on all the Marquette business like her brother. What she thought she noticed earlier though was that Duke didn't have a bodyguard. The brothers did, and Damen's wife Heaven had one.

"Fine. My office, now," Creed snapped, and the two men walked off. Talicia was happy for the reprieve, but she figured it wouldn't be long before Creed would come back and ride her for ducking out to the street. This might be her last night. Aw well, might as well make it count.

Talicia served and smiled all evening until time for closing. Her feet hurt. She was used to standing on them for hours a day as she made the circuit in the club but Marquette's added tension wore her energy away faster. When the last customer thanked Damen over and over then drifted out the door, a waitress locked it. All the while Stefan never stopped playing.

At that point, he tinkled over the keys, making the music dance. Talicia kept her gaze lowered to stacking plates on a table. What she wanted to do was stare at him but didn't dare. A sharp key brought her head up, and he was looking right at her. He mouthed something she couldn't understand then signaled with a finger crooked at her.

Talicia scanned the restaurant, but Creed wasn't around. She peered back at Stefan and shook her head. Again, he signaled.

She denied him.

"Don't make me come get you." The bastard's voice boomed over the mic.

Talicia grumbled and pointed to the dirty dishes. Stefan half stood, and she relented. The man was stubborn. If he got her fired, he was going to hear it from her. Stefan scooted over on the bench just enough for her to have to squeeze beside him, her thigh pressing against his. He could have done better than that, but he just wanted to touch her. Her pointed scowl at him said so, but he winked.

"Did you like the music?" he asked.

"You always ask me that."

"I always want to know what you think."

She glanced down at his fingers and couldn't resist touching them as they moved over the keys. Stefan's hands were far bigger than hers, and she watched as he guided her movements by their touch.

"You're brilliant. At least I think so," she teased, "but not your nephew."

"I'm not surprised. Gideon's got an ear for music."

She tilted her head to the side. "You're not offended?"

He played with one hand and stroked her cheek with

the other. "Why should I be? I'm not playing to be perfect. I'm playing to make my listeners happy. Plus, all I want is happiness, Licia—for me and for everyone around me. I know that sounds like the words of a child."

"No, an optimist. That's you. Dark times come, and they come hard. You can't avoid it."

"And you can't avoid the sunshine either. It sneaks into cracks and crevices to brighten everything."

"See what I said? Optimist." Talicia scooted closer to him without meaning to, and he stopped playing all together to wrap an arm about her waist. For a few precious minutes, she forgot about impressing the Marquettes and just basked in Stefan's embrace.

"I can't wait to get you home," he whispered in her ear. "I'm going to make love to you."

Talicia shivered in delight. She rested a hand on his thigh and snuggled her mouth against the side of his neck. Her body strained to be naked with his, making love just as he suggested. Weariness washed over her, but she had no intention of giving into it. Once she was alone with Stefan, she was going to enjoy every moment.

Reality washed over her when she heard Creed's voice. He wasn't speaking to them, but just the sound tore apart Talicia's world where only she and Stefan existed. She straightened and pushed at his chest. He refused to let her get up, but he gave her space.

Stefan touched a thumb to her bottom lip, but he didn't kiss her. She swayed a bit toward him and caught herself just in time. Disappointment colored his expression, but then he looked past her. When he narrowed his eyes, she looked too. Creed watched them, but he didn't make any kind of signals. Damen walked over and said something to Creed. Then Duke reappeared.

"What's going on?" Stefan wondered.

Talicia groaned. "I think I'm about to get fired. "Your cousin will probably get off scot free, but Creed's not going to give me a second chance."

"What happened?"

"Well, I was outside with Duke and…" She paused, waiting for him to look suspicious or even angry. Nothing. He didn't dislike Duke as Damen did, but he wasn't jealous either. The fact annoyed her a little. "We were out too long when it wasn't time for our break. Creed caught us coming back in, and I just know that's it."

"He's not that anal, honey. Don't worry."

"Since when?"

He chuckled. "You just met him."

"And all I've seen is anal."

"Trust me."

"Stefan, don't try to hang onto my job for me, okay? I have to prove myself. If this is it, I don't care. I can find something else for the time being. If by some miracle it's not, then let me do things my way. Promise me."

"Licia."

"Promise me. I can take care of myself. I've been doing it all these years."

"Yes, and you've had a hard time."

"Because I can't handle it?" A bite rose into her tone she hadn't meant to let loose.

"No, because you were alone. No one should have to battle alone. Period. We all need someone to lean on. I'm here now."

The words of his song echoed in what he said this time. "Stefan, you act like we're going to—"

"Stefan, I need to speak to you," Creed said.

He'd approached them without her noticing. She

hoped he didn't overhear their conversation. The man totally ignored her and focused on his brother.

"Sure." Stefan tapped Talicia's nose. "Stay put. I'll be right back." He squeezed her thigh before he rose, and Creed noticed. The two men walked away and joined Damen and Duke near the kitchen. Then the troupe disappeared through that door. She hoped they weren't going to get into an argument about how soon and the best method of dumping her and her brother on the street.

Talicia glanced toward the exit and noticed both Jerome and one of the other bodyguards stood there. For some reason, she had the feeling they were given an order not to let her out. That contradicted her earlier thought that Creed was getting rid of her. Stefan didn't have the chance to order Jerome to block her, but Creed did. Why should he care?

After stretching her achy muscles, Talicia stood and moved back to the table she'd been cleaning up when Stefan interrupted. Twenty minutes later, Stefan still hadn't returned, so she finished her personal tasks and changed out of the work clothes into what she had worn to the restaurant. She found a bag no one seemed to be using and put the work clothes inside it. When they were clean and dry, she would bring them back, but tomorrow before her shift—if there was a shift—she would get some clothes that actually fit.

Testing her theory about whether she was allowed to leave, Talicia gathered the bag and her purse and headed out toward the front. Right away, Jerome moved into her path. "I'm sorry, Ms. Talicia, you need to wait for Stefan."

"Move out of the way, Jerome. I'm not going home with him tonight." She lied to see what he would do.

Jerome didn't even look at the second man. He

swung his head side to side. "Please, go back into the dining room and wait."

She slapped her hands on her hips. "I'm not a prisoner, you know. Plus, you said you work for me too because I'm his wife!"

"That's right, and my top priority is your safety."

"So what? I can't travel alone anymore?"

"That's not what I'm saying."

"What are you saying, Jerome? Stefan definitely didn't tell you to stop me. He was playing all night."

"True, but like I said your safety comes first. Sometimes I don't do exactly what Stefan tells me if it means going against my primary duty."

She blinked at him. "For real?"

One side of his mouth rose. "Yeah, for real."

Talicia glanced at the other guard and realized he was the one that protected Creed. She had no idea of his name, but this monster looked dangerous. "I wonder how that goes over for him when he tells Creed no."

She waited for the beast to say something, but he remained silent.

"Don't talk much?"

Jerome chuckled. "I'm sure it doesn't happen often, but then again who knows. Mr. Creed is a different breed."

The guard came to life and cut a look at Jerome so dark, he should have dropped dead of a heart attack right there. Jerome was apparently not impressed. However, he did quit talking about Creed. They were loyal, she'd give them that, but maybe they were paid a lot to make sure of it.

"Jerome, look, just tell Stefan or Creed or whoever told you to get in my way that I got the better of you."

Both guards' eyebrows shot up in disbelief. She

couldn't be serious, they said. She moved to the right, but Jerome shifted with her. The door was like inches away, but no dice. Strong arms came around her waist as soon as she was ready to shame Jerome. Stefan's chin touched her shoulder.

"Are you trying to leave me, honey?" He kissed her ear, and she blushed. The damn man had caught her.

"Your bodyguard is stubborn. He seems to think he's responsible for me."

"He is. Come on." Stefan laced his fingers with hers and nodded at Jerome.

The other man went into action right away. "Just one second. Let us check the perimeter."

Talicia looked to Stefan to see if she could glean what all the subterfuge was about, but his expression remained pleasant but closed. Jerome and Creed's man disappeared through the door. A few minutes later, the beast returned and held the door for them. Stefan walked her out and led her to the car Jerome had waiting for them.

Stefan's arm curved around her shoulders in the back seat, and she snuggled into his side. Once they were underway toward home, she questioned him. "Stefan, what's all the caution about? I've never seen Jerome so wound up."

"Don't worry about it, honey."

"Just tell me."

"Maybe when we get home. For now, just relax. Oh, and if you were worried Creed will fire you, forget it. He was a little angry, but just don't go off when you're not on break."

"A little angry?" She snorted.

He looked down at her, and his expression grew serious. "Don't go outside alone again."

"I was right. There is something going on. You better

tell me."

He sighed and ran a hand over the side of her face then kissed her. She strained closer, tingles of desire spreading to every inch of her body. All day no kisses and Stefan so near made her a cranky woman in her own right.

After some time, he raised his head, but Talicia reached up to tug him back down to her. For the moment, she forgot about everything and everyone except for him.

CHAPTER FOURTEEN

Stefan moaned against Talicia's lips, and he cupped her face so he could raise her chin higher. He kissed along her throat and felt her breasts pushing against his chest. The smallest of tremors rocked shook her, and she shut her eyes in complete surrender to him. Yet, he kept one eye on the passing scenery. If she saw how distracted he was, she would start questioning him again. He managed to make her forget about what was going on when he kissed her and ran a hand over her back down to her ass.

His wife moaned his name, but he had to pull away. She sidetracked him with his desire for her. There would be time enough to take Talicia once he got her home safe. For now, he couldn't think straight. Some bastard had gotten close to her on the street, pretending to be drunk. If Duke hadn't been there, he didn't know what would have happened. Stefan had never been so grateful for his cousin's training in his life.

Earlier, Stefan had approached Creed and Damen expecting to hear complaints about Talicia, which he fully intended to defend her against. "What's going on with you two?" he'd asked. "If you think you're going to fire her, Creed, then—"

"It's got nothing to do with that." Creed sighed and ran a hand through his hair. "My office."

The four of them had trooped to the back, and Stefan took a seat on the opposite side of Creed's desk, while Duke and Damen remained standing. Stefan knew he appeared calm, but something told him the situation was serious.

Creed didn't keep him wondering for long. "Someone tried to grab Talicia out front."

Stefan knocked over his chair as he jumped to his feet. "What?"

"Calm down," Creed ordered. "It didn't look like it to her. As far as she knows, he was some drunkard."

"How can you be sure?" Stefan wrestled with the decision to go out to the dining room to look Talicia over for himself. However, he had just left her there. He sat close to her, and she seemed fine.

"I gave the order that she's not allowed out," Creed went on. "Don't worry. She's not getting past Jerome, let alone Pete."

Stefan was tempted to say Creed didn't know Talicia like he did, but he changed his mind. Yes, she was strong, but his beautiful wife wouldn't be able to stand against the bodyguard. He also wasn't worried that either man would hurt her. She was in good hands while he got to the bottom of what was going on.

"Anyway," Creed said, "Duke made sure she didn't know how serious it was."

Stefan faced Duke. "*Was* it serious?"

Duke nodded. "Yeah, I'm not a fool. I know when a man's drunk and when he's faking. That guy was faking all the way, which gives rise to the question of why. I gave him a hit that didn't do as much damage as I expected.

He couldn't have taken that blow unless he was guarded against it."

Stefan swore.

"There's no need to panic yet," Damen told them. "We don't know it wasn't just some jerk wanting to get in her panties or if he attacked her because of us.'

"What are you saying?" Creed snapped. "We haven't had any incidents in a while. I say it's too coincidental to her situation. It's likely someone spilled about who you are, Stefan, and they decided she was hiding out with you. In all the time you played at the club, didn't you think about being recognized?"

"I did but…" He let his voice trail off. He had never used his real name except with Talicia and Tyjon. The entire time, he realized he was being foolish, but it had never stopped him going. After she and he became lovers, logic hadn't entered his head.

"But you wanted to perform," Creed growled. "Singing at Marquette's wasn't good enough."

"Lay off him, Creed," Damen said. "We have a potential situation. It might be nothing. Like I said, the incident could end with running that guy off, and we'll hear no more about it."

"I'm not that convinced. Have either of you considered this might be all in Talicia's plan? Destroy the club, get a firmer hold on Stefan, and force him to reveal her existence?"

"Ouch." Duke winced. "Even I felt the winter breeze coming off that comment, cuz."

Stefan didn't say a word.

"Aren't you going to say anything, Stefan?"

Stefan took his time standing to face his oldest brother. "You seem to think I'm some airheaded fool who can't figure out when a woman is using me."

"I never said that. You must admit you've never brought a woman around. Duke, the fool, thought you were gay."

"Hey," Duke called out, but he chuckled. "Anybody could have made that mistake."

"So what?" Stefan hated talking about Talicia with his brothers behind her back. She deserved better. "I know people a hell of a lot better than you three do."

Damen squeezed his shoulder in an effort to calm him no doubt. "But you're taken with her, Stefan. Admit it. Your eyes followed her the whole night, and we know that little song you sang was for her."

Duke snorted. "Even if it did make her bolt out of the restaurant like the devil chased her."

Heat suffused Stefan's cheeks. He'd seen her run too. She fought him a lot less than she fought everyone else, but she still kept him at arm's length. He never intended to keep the marriage going, but from the time she entered his house, he knew he wanted her to stay. Did that mean he cared about her more than he first thought? The prospect seemed unlikely, but he didn't doubt it. There was no denying Talicia consumed his thoughts.

Creed rolled his shoulders. "Talicia may or may not be in real trouble. The fact is we can't be too careful. So, we up security tonight and see if there's a repeat. Is that agreeable to you two?"

Stefan agreed, and so did his brother Damen.

"What am I chopped liver?" Duke asked. "I was the one that protected your little sweetheart."

"Thank you," Stefan said with emphasis. "I mean it."

"Any time. It was fun teasing her. She's got a lot of fire."

"She does," Stefan agreed. "Licia is an unbelievable woman."

All three of them stared at him, and his face grew hot again. Creed was right in saying he never brought his lovers around. That was his way. He liked to keep his private life private, and he wasn't the playboy that Damen was before he married.

They spoke a little longer, discussing the details of leaving the restaurant for the night. Because they had gone through several incidents in the past decade of people trying to get to one of them, Stefan and his brothers knew the drill. They also trusted their bodyguards to be able to handle the situation and to move smoothly through the process of leaving the restaurant for the night.

"I'm going out ahead of you," Stefan had told the others. "Licia is probably tired, and after all she's gone through, I want her to be as relaxed as possible."

He finished up with his brothers, and now he and Talicia were in the car heading home. Stefan believed they were fine with just a few more miles to go, but he stayed on alert and tugged Talicia closer to him.

The first indication that his assumptions were all wrong was at the sound of the back window shattering. Something whizzed by his ear and burned his skin.

"Get down," Jerome shouted.

Stefan twisted in his seat, taking Talicia with him. He landed on top of her on the floor and pressed her down. She clutched at his shoulders, already shaking hard. "It's okay. We're okay, Licia."

Her nails dug through the material of his shirt and sank into his shoulders. He winced but didn't move. The car swerved and dipped to one side. He was pretty sure a couple tires had gone flat.

In the front seat, Jerome was shouting into his phone. "We've been shot at. They're not behind us, but I don't know if they'll be back. Bring two men, and meet us now!"

The line was disconnected, and Jerome dialed again. This time, Stefan knew he called his brothers. He started to sit up, but Talicia screamed and held onto him. "No, Stefan, don't. If they hurt you…"

He gazed down at her and was shocked to find tears streaming down the sides of her face. Of course this was an intense situation and he shouldn't have expected anything else. The fear was what tore his gut apart. Talicia wasn't just afraid for herself. She was terrified of him being hurt.

"Please, don't," she begged. "I can't…Stefan, stay down."

He kissed her lips then turned his head. "Jerome, I don't want my brothers to get it into their heads to come out here."

"They won't," Jerome called back, but they should know. "Mr. Creed didn't believe it, did he?"

Stefan tensed. "Later."

"Yes, sir."

The car seemed to speed up then slow down and finally stop. Stefan tugged his wife to his chest and ran hands over her length to be sure she was fine. In the spot where Jerome had stopped, there were no streetlights, so he couldn't see Talicia clearly. He was glad because she wouldn't notice the blood he felt dripping down his ear.

Jerome's door opened, and he stepped out. Through a gap between the seat and the doorframe, Stefan noticed his bodyguard pull a gun from somewhere and hold it at the ready.

"Anything?" Stefan called.

"Nothing. I think it was a scare tactic."

Talicia started under him. He felt for her face. "Okay,

honey?"

"No."

"You're hurt?" His gut clenched. "Where?"

"No, I mean, I'm so sorry, Stefan. This is all my fault. If I never met you, it wouldn't have happened."

"Shh, quiet. This isn't your fault, Licia. In a way, it's mine. I shouldn't have thought I could get away with performing at the club without consequences. I'm not going to get down on myself either. I can live the life I choose to. If anyone's really to blame, it's the greedy men who don't know how to work legally for what they want."

"Stefan, did you get hurt?" He heard the worry in her tone, but he didn't want to lie to her.

"Everything's fine, Licia."

"Stop saying that! All that glass, and you were so fast. I can't stand the thought of you being hurt."

"I know. Shh. Rest easy."

Another car arrived, and Talicia put him in a death grip. Then she took a deep breath, and on the smallest of whimpers, she started searching the floor for something.

"What are you looking for?" he whispered.

"My bag. I have a knife. If they try anything, I'm not going down easy."

Her hand closed over her purse, and he laid his atop hers. "No."

"Stefan."

"It's not an enemy. It's backup."

When the other car stopped, men's voices filled the night air. Stefan recognized the guards he had hired to watch his house. Jerome opened the back door and leaned in. "Both of you okay?"

"We're fine," Stefan said. "Safe to sit up?"

"Yeah, but let's move fast. I don't like being out here in the opening."

They transferred to the new car. As they moved, Stefan made sure the car Jerome had driven was blocked from Talicia's view. He knew it was a mess, and she didn't need to relive it with a visual.

"Get us home fast, Jerome."

Behind the wheel of the new car with a guard sitting across from him and another on Stefan's other side, Jerome peeled away from the curb. "Stefan, it's been suggested that I take you to Creed's place."

"And put them at risk?"

Jerome met his gaze in the rearview mirror. "It's easier to guard you all if you're going to the same house. Then we can use more men to begin the search."

Talicia sat forward. "What do you mean begin the search? We need to call the police."

Stefan tried pulling her to his side again, but she resisted. He knew he'd be in for an argument if he didn't explain. "The police haven't been able to handle things up until now."

She looked at him. "So you all are taking it into your own hands? Is that what rich people do?"

He didn't respond, and she flopped back against the seat. Stefan reached for her hand, but she moved it out of reach. Talking to her did nothing. She sat as a statue at his side, obviously angry but more afraid. The look in her eyes, the trembling, he knew she fought her emotions with everything she had.

"Licia," he whispered, hating it when she didn't speak to him. She didn't answer, and he squeezed her fingers gently between his. "Honey."

A shuddering sigh shook her shoulders. "Stefan, this isn't you, is it? You're okay with hunting down people and killing them?"

"I'm not going to do the hunting myself."

"But you're sending men out?"

"Yes."

"Why? The police—"

"Aren't good enough," he growled. She stared wide-eyed at him, and he drew her into his arms, this time by force. Stefan shoved her head to his shoulder and stroked the back of her head. "Do you think for a minute I'm such a nice guy that I'll let a man try to kill you and then walk away?"

She clutched his shirt. "But..."

"But nothing." He pushed her back to look into her eyes. "I don't know what's going to happen between us in the next week or month or year. If you're going to live in peace whether it's with me or away from me—" His voice wavered at those words because he already knew he didn't want her gone from his life, ever. "—then nothing and no one can threaten you."

"That's unrealistic. I mean not the crazy drug dealer part because he was real, but there have been people in my life who thought they could put their hands on me."

"And I'll make them sorry for it."

She grinned. "Thanks, but I got it."

"*I've* got it," he insisted. "Anyway, this situation is different. From the way you're shaking you haven't had to deal with it before. I'm handling it the way me and my family see fit. I'm sorry you don't like that."

She grumbled. "I never knew you were so stubborn. It's like I don't know you."

"Well, I'll give you plenty of time to get to know me." He kissed her, and he was happy she didn't turn her head away. "Just hold on. This will all be over soon."

CHAPTER FIFTEEN

Talicia sat in Shada's kitchen at her and Creed's house. She couldn't believe she was in the same room with the woman, let alone having stayed at their place. The restaurant was closed for the day, and most of the Marquette men were in what they called a billiard room. Damen had gone to dog his wife's steps at her job. Talicia didn't have anything to do except ring her hands and wish she'd been able to get some sleep the night before. At least Stefan had thought to arrange to pick up Tyjon. That beauty queen was still in his room.

"If you want, I can help make breakfast for the guys," Talicia offered. She was by no means a cook, but since Shada wasn't calling her a bitch and telling her to get out, she figured she could make an effort.

"Why would I need help in my own kitchen?" was the snarky reply. Talicia sighed.

Upon closer inspection of the woman, Talicia noticed the dark rings around her eyes. So she hadn't slept either. Talicia wondered if it had to do with the shooting or just being pregnant. After all, they had been trying to kill her not Creed. Then again Stefan could have been hurt, and they all seemed to adore him. She didn't blame them.

Shada stood at the refrigerator with her back turned, heaved her shoulders, and then turned. "Look, Creed's overprotectiveness means I can't cook at the restaurant even though I have months to go before dropping this load. The only time I get to do it freely is here. So I don't like sharing my kitchen."

"Okay."

Shada piled ingredients for the meal on the island counter, and Talicia drummed her fingers on the surface. Shada glared at her, and she stopped.

"I don't cook anyway."

The other woman blinked at her. "At all?"

"Not really. I live with my brother, and he's the cook in our place."

"Hmm."

Talicia frowned. "You're thinking how much of a woman can I be. Well, I'm plenty woman. I know I don't look like much, but—"

"For real?"

"What do you mean for real?" Talicia snapped.

Shada set the green pepper she held on the counter and moved around it. Her chocolate gaze studied Talicia, and she frowned. Talicia stiffened but backed up. Shada stopped advancing on her, and she breathed a sigh of relief.

"You really don't think much of yourself?"

Talicia realized what she'd sounded like. "Of course I do. I'm damn good at my job. I made my club into a successful business when my partner couldn't be bothered. Everything I know about accounting, marketing, business in general, I taught myself. No, I'm not rolling in money, but I'm damn sure not about to land on the street. Even if I did I'd—"

"Whoa." Shada laughed. "I get it. That's not what I meant."

Talicia put her hands on her hips. "Then what did you mean?"

"Your looks."

A hand flew to her hair before Talicia could catch herself. She smoothed the strands in place. Damn it if she was so self-conscious about it, why the hell did she cut it? She couldn't have explained it if anyone asked.

Shada's hair was messy from just rising, but it was freshly permed and swept up in a mid-length ponytail. Soft tendrils had escaped the band and curled around her face, making her look more beautiful than if she'd just come from the salon. A pang of jealousy touched Talicia when her gaze lowered to the woman's fuller figure. She wondered if she would gain weight and get bigger boobs if she got pregnant.

What the heck am I thinking?

Shada shrugged and turned away. "I'm going to tell you the truth. I hate your guts. I've never seen the brothers like this."

"So they're not usually like the mob?"

"What?" Shada frowned at her.

"Never mind."

"I can tell you're not after Stefan's money. Still, you have to admit you're bad news. Last night he could have been killed. Stefan is the sweetest man. I love Creed to death, but I don't mind admitting Stefan is beyond genuine. He doesn't deserve someone like you. I pictured him with this innocent little thing who thinks he hung the moon and hangs on his every word."

"Not me who punched your husband and—" She cut herself off because she'd been about to blab how she fought Stefan the night he barged in on her and Kevin.

That's all she needed. If she told Shada, the woman would think she abused Stefan and probably cut her with the knife she sliced the peppers with.

To tell the truth, her feelings were hurt. Here she was thinking she would try, and it didn't even mean anything. She was too hard-edged, and the issue with Colby made matters a million times worse.

"So what you're saying is you're never going to accept me?" Talicia asked, even though she already knew the answer.

"You're Stefan's wife, but I don't have to sleep with you. Just stay out of my face."

"We're agreed," Talicia said and saluted. She spun on her heel and walked out of the kitchen. By the time she reached the room she and Stefan had been assigned, she had a raging migraine and a stomach ache. She sat on the side of the bed and stared at the bag that had been brought from Stefan's house with her things. If she wanted, she could pack it and walk out the door. No one would notice or miss her except Stefan. He would get over it eventually.

Talicia considered the plan. She could disappear and let the insurance company know to give her portion of the money to her brother when the time came. Tyjon could support himself from it for a long while.

"Who am I kidding?"

She couldn't leave her brother, not with Colby looking for them. Stefan showed his stubborn nature last night, which meant he wouldn't give up searching for her either. He was determined to do things his way, and she was going to fall in line. Oh, he wasn't mean like Creed, but Shada didn't know him like Talicia was learning about him. Stefan was that arrogant man's brother after all and had the same stubborn, bossy genes.

Talicia stood and stripped the clothes she had donned that morning. She stepped into the shower and turned the temperature as hot as she could stand it. Then for the first time in so long, she let go. She sobbed nonstop for what felt like hours. Her heart seemed to shatter, and she sagged against the wall of the shower, shaking, sick, cold, and hot all at the same time.

When arms came around her, she started and tried to pull away. Stefan wouldn't let her. He turned her by her shoulders to face him and plastered her wet body to his. He was naked, but she couldn't think of him sexually at that moment. All the energy in her had drained away. Clinging to him for dear life and willing herself to pull it together, she cried harder.

"Stefan," she murmured into his chest.

"Go ahead and cry, honey. As much as you need to."

"Don't encourage me."

His fingers danced over her spine in a gentle caress. Then he cupped the back of her head. She whimpered. He raised her up and wrapped both her legs around his waist. For a long time, they remained beneath the spray. When her fingertips wrinkled, Stefan turned off the water and stepped out of the shower still holding her. He didn't let her down but did his best to dry them both.

"You're crazy," she muttered.

He carried her into the bedroom and lay on the bed with her. Talicia snuggled against his side. She sneezed and shivered, and like a protective bear, he jerked the tucked sheets out from beneath the mattress and cocooned her in them.

"Do you want to talk about it?" he asked.

"Not really."

She waited for him to push, but he said nothing. A sudden urge to come clean and let the chips fall where they may came over her. If the two of them weren't going to make it, at least he would know.

"I'm not an innocent little thing who thinks you hung the moon and hangs onto your every word."

He screwed up his face. "Was there a question of that?"

"No, I mean I'm not the ideal."

"Who's ideal?"

"Yours or…anyone else's." She lowered her gaze because it was getting stuffy in there, and it had nothing to do with the sheets. Creed liked the A/C on full blast, so the covering was welcome.

"If my brother said something he shouldn't have, honey, tell me. I'll have another talk with him."

"You can talk until you're blue in the face. It won't matter, Stefan. What they all think of me is what they will always think of me."

"You don't know that. I happen to believe they'll come to love you. They've already started to accept your presence in my life."

"Um, no they haven't. You're delusional."

He sat up and drew her higher on the bed to lie between his legs. Talicia leaned on his chest. She traced fingertips along the goose bumps on his arms, but he didn't seem to notice the cold. That was white people, she assumed.

"You seem to think *I'm* the innocent little thing that hangs on your every word person," Stefan complained. "Do you know how many years I've been fighting against that image? Damen and Creed both think of me that way, a fragile person who can be broken and who needs pampering. Just because I look on the bright side, I'm weak?"

"I don't think you're weak. It's just the short end the

youngest gets. Tyjon likes to call me baby sister, and I know we're twins, but he is a few minutes younger." She laughed. "I think of him as my little brother, and therefore I have to look out for him."

"Have you ever considered letting him be a man?"

She gasped.

"Talicia, I don't mean to offend you." He held up his hands like he was scared she'd get mad. She was offended and a little angry, but she knew what he said was true. Tyjon *should* take care of himself.

"My dad used to try every trick to get Tyjon to man up."

"He beat him?"

"No. Everything but that. Nothing he did was good enough or strong enough. I started getting in between them almost from day one. Then we went to school, and it was worse."

Stefan stiffened. "How?"

"Boys started beating him up because he was so soft and acted like a girl. You know Tyjon. The way he is now is the way he always was, even as a kid. Way over the top, loud, with a look at me attitude. It got his ass beat in the ghetto on the regular."

"Kids can be cruel. I'm sorry, Talicia."

"Thanks." A lump rose in her throat remembering, but she wanted to tell him everything. "We are both really small built, and we were skinner and shorter back then. I tried to stick up for him, but they kept throwing me aside and hurting my baby brother. You have to understand what it was like seeing him swollen and bruised every day telling me, 'It's all right, Licia. I'm going to get them next time.' In a way, he's like you. He smiles a lot, always sunny. But I think Tyjon's attitude back then was an act."

"Why do you say that?"

"Because one day I heard him crying in his room. I ran in and asked him what was wrong. He said why did he have to turn out like he was. Why couldn't he be strong like our father? Why him?"

Talicia's voice cracked, and she slapped a hand over her mouth. Stefan's arms surrounded her, and he pulled her tight to his chest. She refused to give into crying again. He had already seen enough of her blubbering for a lifetime.

"Didn't anyone help him?"

"Funny enough, my dad recalled what it meant to be a father. He went up to the school to talk to the principal, and he even started getting off work earlier so he could walk us home. That was nice."

"I have the feeling it didn't end there."

"No."

"I got boobs, and a bit of ass. Then my dad died."

"Huh?"

She laughed because she'd said it vague like that on purpose. His confused look was worth it. "What's your body have to do with it?"

Talicia drew her knees to her chest. "Where I come from the minute a girl starts looking more like a girl, the boys start pulling on her, thinking they can touch whenever they get ready."

"Licia." His voice grew so tight she realized her mistake and whirled to face him.

"Calm down, Stefan. It's not what you think. I was never forced into anything."

"You're not lying to me?"

"No. It's the truth. I said grabbed like a smack on the butt, a pinch in the wrong place. Plus I was never dumb enough to walk anywhere alone. When my dad died, we were unprotected again because my mother had to work twice as hard to take care of Tyjon and me. That's when I knew it was up to me."

"What did you do?"

Talicia lost her nerve. She didn't want to tell him. In a way, it could have been much worse than it was, but she couldn't be sure of Stefan's reaction. Would he look at her differently or think less of her?

Someone knocked on the door, and she breathed a sigh of relief. "Who is it?"

"Mr. Stefan, Mrs. Talicia," came the lilt of a Hispanic woman's voice, "breakfast is served."

Talicia frowned in confusion at Stefan. "I thought they didn't have a maid."

"They do, but she doesn't cook at all." Stefan grinned. "Not unless she wants to incur Shada's wrath.

"Ahh." Talicia started to tell Stefan to go down without her that she wasn't hungry. He took her hand when he slid to the edge of the bed to guide her to her feet. A rush of love washed over her, and she didn't want to let him go just yet.

The two of them dressed, and Talicia peeked into the mirror at her hair. Without gel, the short spikes stood straight up. At least they were permed, so it wasn't a big dry fuzz ball. She ran a hand over them but to no avail. Behind her, Stefan watched her. She followed the line of his sight and found the man staring at her boobs.

"Don't you have a bra?" he asked. "There a lot of men in the house.

She bit her lip to hide a grin. So Mr. Stefan was jealous after all. Hah, even skinny she had a little something. At least she did in her husband's eyes. "Not with me. They're small. It's fine. No one will notice."

"They're men." He pulled open a drawer where she had dumped her clothes last night when she was

exhausted. “Here, wear this.”

Talicia took the shirt from his hands and stuffed it back into the drawer then grabbed his hand. “Come on. I’m hungry.”

The walked together down into the lion’s den.

CHAPTER SIXTEEN

Conversation flowed around Stefan, but he focused on his wife. He couldn't take his eyes off her long enough to pay attention to what was said at the table. When he found Talicia crying, his heart splintered. He'd never seen her so broken, but he had known it was coming. She was on edge and hurting. He saw it in her eyes and did everything he could to be there for her.

Curiosity made Stefan wonder what she had to share with him about her past, but he also knew it didn't matter. Not the innocent type to hang on his words? Well, he didn't need her to hang on his words, but in a way, Talicia's heart was as innocent as they came. No one saw it, and he didn't believe it was just wishful thinking on his part.

Talicia. He spoke her name in his head, and a startling truth came through with amazing clarity. Why didn't he see it before? His sweet Talicia, his wife, she needed him. Stefan was sure of it, however, far more than that, he loved her. For the first time, he realized it. Lust wasn't what he felt in that shower when he came across her naked and crying. What he felt was an intense need to protect her, to take her in his arms and never let anyone near her again. No one who could do her harm.

"Stefan, what are staring at?" she whispered, leaning close to him. "If it's my boobs, I told you no one noticed."

She was wrong. One of the guards had looked, and a flash of anger came over Stefan like he had never experienced. Jerome, always anticipating him, had shuffled the guy out of sight. Since then, Stefan found reasons to lean in front of her and block the view. She'd tossed him looks that said she knew what he was doing and was amused. The woman had no idea how cute she was, so tiny a man felt the need to shelter her.

"Stefan," Creed snapped. "Are you in on this conversation? It does have to do with your wife."

"What about my wife?" he asked, focusing at last.

"We were thinking of sending her and her brother—"

"No."

Creed's eyebrows rose at Stefan's tone. Stefan cleared his throat. Duke crowed, and Damen laughed. Under the table, Stefan took Talicia's hand in his. Down the table a couple seats, Tyjon made eyes at one of the guards. The man blushed, apparently not put off by Talicia's brother.

Stefan focused on his own brother's angry face. "Licia stays with me. There's no discussion about that."

Creed grumbled. "You have to think about what's best for this family."

"I'm thinking about what's best for *my* family. My immediate one, and that's Talicia. You can't tell me you would send Shada away if she was in danger."

"I would if it meant she would be more protected and…damn it, this isn't about me and Shada." He wasn't able to finish the lie, and Shada had looked at him like he had gone crazy. Everyone knew his brother was nuts about his fiancée, and Stefan had hoped one day to have a similar feeling about the woman he married. He couldn't have known it would happen so soon.

At his side, Talicia squeezed his hand. "If it will mean Stefan is safe, I don't mind going away. In fact, I think it's a good idea. Tyjon and I can just pick somewhere. I have a little money in the bank, so I can take care of us. Not a big deal."

All around the table, Stefan's family was agreeing with her. Even Tyjon reluctantly came on board with the suggestion. "I'll miss the lap of luxury y'all live in. Imma tell you the truth!" Tyjon pouted and gazed around the dining room as if he worked to commit it all to memory. "My sis being safe is more important, and I think it's time for me to look out for her for once. Don't you worry about us, boo boo. We will be just fine."

Discussion broke out, suggestions flew around the room of where Talicia and Tyjon should go and how the operation should be handled to have them transported without anyone in New Orleans knowing about it.

Stefan raised his fork without considering what he ate. He chewed, swallowed, and wiped his mouth. When he was done, he excused himself from the table. In the hall, he had a brief conversation with Jerome and then headed up to the bedroom. Some moments later, Talicia entered the room, and Stefan pulled her into his arms for a kiss.

When he let her up for a breath of air, she rested her hands on his chest. "Stefan, you know us going is for the best, right? Everyone seemed like they ganged up on you, and I didn't make it any better, but this is my fault, and I have to make it right."

"Tell me how it's your fault?" he said, even though they had had this conversation.

"Because I tricked Colby."

"What do you mean?"

"I pretended to give in to his threats, but I as soon as the drugs were delivered, I took them."

His eyes widened. "You did what?"

"I took them, and I turned them in to the police. I thought it was going to be some small time stuff, like individual buyers. He was trading with resellers. That fool thought my club was going to be Grand Central."

"Licia."

"What?"

He drew her closer. "Honey, you probably lost him millions."

Her mouth hung open.

"If the police had been able to do a sting, they could have gotten him and the drugs with evidence that would stand up in court."

"How do you know?"

He shrugged. "TV, talking to the guys."

What Stefan didn't say was that he had discussed it Jerome, who knew more about that world. He'd come from it before he decided to go straight with his life. Jerome had speculated on why Colby would keep coming after Talicia and destroy the club he had wanted to do business in. Likely, there was someone above him looking for their money. Now that Colby knew Talicia had ties with the Marquettes, he expected the man to try to get his hands on her and demand ransom. Stefan had no intention of letting that happen.

"Stefan, what's with the bags? This one is yours."

"I know."

She stared at him. "You're not planning on coming with us, are you?"

"I am."

"Stefan, you can't. Please, it's too dangerous. Plus, the arrangements haven't been made yet. We were talking tomorrow."

"Honey, do you think I agreed with my brother downstairs? I chose not to argue with him or the others. You aren't leaving my side. End of discussion. I'm taking a leave of absence from the restaurant starting today, and we are flying to Costa Rica."

"Costa what? Stefan!"

"Licia, I'd much rather you shout my name when I'm making love to you. Not when you think I will change my mind. I've made my decision."

"I can't believe you're acting like this. It's not your decision. You're not going."

"You're my wife, and we go together."

"Don't pull that." She folded her arms over her chest. "I don't care how stubborn you think you are, I'm more so, and I say your ass is staying here."

He narrowed his eyes at her.

"I'm sorry. I didn't mean to cuss at you. Look, Stefan. I lo—care about you. It's killing me that I'm risking your life. I know you love your family, and I don't want to hurt them either and cause you heartache."

"What about the heartache I'll feel losing my wife?"

She went silent for a minute. "D-don't joke."

He wasn't ready to confess his love since he had just discovered it for himself. She might not feel the same, but he would do everything in his power to change that fact. Helping Talicia to fall in love with him would be his primary objective after the danger had passed.

"Licia, I will follow you if you try to leave me. Which course of action do you think will work better for us, going together, or me risking exposing myself to find you?"

"You're playing dirty."

"I'll get into the mud to keep you."

"You're infuriating, you know that? Your bothers have no clue how manipulative you are. I should go right downstairs and tell them."

He chuckled. "Feel free."

She grumbled, but he pulled her to him and spun her around so he could trap her in his arms. His little wife wiggled so satisfyingly against his thigh, and he hefted her off her feet to enjoy spooning her ass. She stopped fighting when she felt his hard-on. Too late for that. He was going to have her under him before they left.

"Costa Rica," he whispered in her ear to settle her some, "warm all year around, monkeys."

She laughed. "Wait, that's your selling point?"

"To get a laugh. It worked."

He heard her sigh and relaxed a bit himself. For too long, she'd been wound tight. Even at the club, he sensed it. While Stefan hated what happened back there, he saw it as a positive as well. Talicia needed to unhook from all the responsibility and to begin to believe she was free to do whatever she wanted. He planned to show her a life where she could breathe easier and stop being afraid.

Stefan carried Talicia to the bed and laid her gently down. He stretched out beside her and ran a finger along her face. His heart swelled again as he thought about how he felt for her. He had to duck his head to keep her from seeing the emotion in his eyes. She would guess his feelings, and it might scare her even more.

"Stefan?"

He kissed her belly through her clothes and then snaked a hand under her shirt. "Hmm?"

She rested a hand over his to still him. "I want to tell you the rest before we do anything."

"I'd rather talk later and make love to you now."

"Please?"

He sat up. "Okay. Come here, and let me hold you."

"Um, can I pace? I feel agitated."

He let her go, and the space beside him seemed like a barren wasteland. Stefan watched her stride back and forth, bottom lip caught between her teeth, hands clenched into fists. Always warring, he thought.

"We were small like I said, and neither one of us knew how to fight. I don't know how many times I was thrown aside when they were going after Tyjon, or pinned when some idiot wanted to cop a feel. Don't get me wrong, I'd kneed a few and put them on the ground, but I wanted more defense."

He nodded his understanding, encouraging her to continue. She twisted her hands together.

"There was this one boy."

"How old were you?"

She winced. "Thirteen."

"Go on."

"He was huge, *really* huge, but he was our age. Most of the kids were smaller than he was, and he thought that equaled him bullying all the smaller kids."

"That always seems to be the way."

"Yeah, immaturity does that. He used to mess with Tyjon too, but I noticed something."

"What?" Stefan wouldn't have been surprised if she told him the bully picked on Tyjon because he liked him. Kids tended to show their feelings in the worst way, like hurting their crush.

"He never actually beat up Tyjon. He just pushed him around and called him names."

Stefan made a noise of understanding, knowing where this was going.

"But I would catch him looking at me a lot when he thought I didn't see him."

"Oh."

She frowned. "What do you mean, oh? He couldn't like me?"

"I thought you were going to say he was gay."

She laughed. "Okay, that makes sense, but no such luck. Anyway, if he liked me, then maybe I could use him. You have to understand I was desperate an—"

"You don't have to justify your actions, Licia. I'm starting to get the picture about how hard life was for you. I thought my brothers and I had a hard time growing up. In a way, we did, but it doesn't lessen anyone else's challenges for them. I'm not judging you, honey, no matter what you tell me."

He was glad he said it because she drifted back to him and climbed onto the bed to let him hold her.

"Ah, that's better, where you belong."

She smacked his arm but settled closer. "I got him alone and told him I'd be his girlfriend if he'd teach me to fight and help me to get strong."

Stefan got why she hesitated to explain. Talicia had in essence sold her body to protect her brother and herself. He meant what he said about not judging her, but it pierced his heart to think there were no adults who could have made sure she never had to go that far.

"It's not as tragic as it sounds." She gave a wry laugh. "That fool was thirteen after all. We held hands, kissed a little, and did a bit of stroking here and there. Turned out he was the stereotypical bully, a coward at heart. He never mustered the courage to go all the way for two years."

Stefan ground his teeth. He didn't want to hear about her having sex with anyone else. Still, he kept his mouth shut.

"In the meantime, I learned to throw a punch, and lifting weights with him meant I grew stronger. Much later, I started taking classes in self-defense and boxing. Now, not many men can beat me, and I've taken down some really big guys."

"You must be proud."

"No, not really." She sat up and drew her knees to her chest. "To be honest, Stefan, I wish I could go back and it all was different. I like myself. Don't get me wrong. I'm glad I stood on my own two feet, and I probably will never fully give in to letting anyone else take care of me."

Stefan didn't miss the way she cut her eyes at him when she said it. *Wanna bet?*

"But on some levels, I… oh, wow, I'm so embarrassed to say this." She smacked a hand over her eyes and ducked her head. "I wish I was more girly. There I said it."

"You don't have to wish. Just do it."

She looked at him. "Everyone would think—"

"Does it matter what they think?"

"What about you?" She lowered her gaze and picked at the sheet under them. "You went for me when I was all tough and angry. My hair is so short, I look like a boy. I'm rail thin, and the curves I do have wouldn't show unless I have a skintight outfit on, which I don't wear. In fact, I'm surprised you noticed I was a woman that first night we met. I mean except for my tone of voice and my name."

"If you're hinting that I'm gay…"

Her mouth dropped open and eyes went wide. "Never! Oh wow, I didn't realize that's how it sounded. No, Stefan, you're all hetero. I'm sorry if I gave the impression I was saying that about you. I don't think that way."

He grinned. "I was teasing you. The one thing I know

about myself is I'm not easily offended. People can say and think what they want. I already know how you see me. You're much more feminine than you think, or anyone who doesn't know you well. You know what, Licia?"

She blushed. "What?"

"The night I met you, I saw your eyes first. Deep brown, wide, and innocent."

She pursed her lips. "I'm so not innocent."

"You are because you don't realize your womanliness. It's as if you haven't discovered the deepest parts of yourself."

"Maybe you're imagining things."

"Am I? You said you wish you were more feminine. What does that make you?"

She hesitated. "It makes me a woman. All woman."

"Maybe you've made certain choices to avoid being hurt."

"Like cut my hair. I regret it so much. I thought I liked it really short. I just kept hacking it off every time it started to get long enough to curl. I didn't wear dresses, but I have to admit I love that one dress you bought me. It makes me mad that I left it at the house."

"I'll buy you a lot more."

She tried to hide a smile and muttered something about buying them herself. He knew it gave her a thrill to have someone willing to care for her, even if she fought him. Stefan planned to spend a great deal of time teaching her what she meant to him and convincing her it was okay to let go.

"Stefan," she breathed after a few moments. Her chest rose and fell as if she were all of a sudden out of breath.

"Easy, honey, what is it?"

"I…I want to tell you something else."

He steeled himself. "Is it bad?"

"No, not really. Well not for me, but for you, who knows."

"I want you to always feel you can tell me anything."

She faced him with an earnest expression. "Where are we going in our marriage? Are we together just because of that whim thing? Because if we are, we can at least get a legal separation. I'll sign a form that says I will never demand any money from you if that's what you want."

"That's not what I want."

She sighed. "I'm saying I don't want to burden you, but I do need to know what we're doing. I don't want to admit it, but it hurts to think when Colby is caught or dead, I won't see you anymore."

A huge grin spread over Stefan's face, and as much as he tried, he couldn't dim it.

"Stefan! I'm serious. This isn't a laughing matter. I need to know."

"You need to know what, honey?" He leaned closer to her until their lips almost touched. She seemed resistant to turning her head away, which he didn't mind at all. "Whether I love you?"

To his supreme satisfaction and surprise, she trembled at the word love. He had thought to spend time showing her his love in the hope that one day she would come to love him. Arrogance had made him think he already knew so much about Talicia. He had missed the most obvious thing and what he desired above all else.

Stefan captured Talicia's chin and raised it before he kissed her long and deep. He wrapped an arm about her shoulders and plastered her lovely body to his. While his cock throbbed in his pants, he ignored it. Right now, he had to get a couple issues straight.

"Licia, do you love me?"

"I…" She tried to pull away, but he held on.

"Because I love you very much."

Her jaw went slack. "Stefan, you're not just saying that to keep me from running off alone, are you?"

"If I didn't love you, would I fight so hard to keep you? Talicia Clay, I love you beyond reason. I want to be with you and have you in my arms every single day. I want you to change your name to Marquette so I can claim you before the entire world."

"Oh boy, oh boy." Her voice quivered. "All that did was make me a shaky mess. I'm so embarrassed, happy, and nervous all at the same time."

She rung her hands and looked everywhere but at him. He burst out laughing. Never had he seen a woman behave so oddly at a declaration of love. Of course Talicia would. She was all woman, but she hadn't allowed herself to be one except in bed. He captured her wild hands and held them against her thighs. With her back against his chest, he nuzzled her cheek and shut his eyes. At last, she began to settle down and turned her face into his.

"I love you," she whispered against his skin. Her breath warmed his face while her words fired up his heart.

"Say it again, please, with my name."

She smiled. "I love you, Stefan, very much. I want to be your wife in every way."

"That's my girl. So you won't run from me?"

"Nope. Never."

"And you will take my name?"

"Yes. Talicia Marquette. It has a nice ring it."

"Absolutely."

CHAPTER SEVENTEEN

Talicia touched her husband's face. He stretched above her on his hands and knees, staring into her eyes. Stefan was so sexy and so muscular. Wonder of wonders he was hers. Talicia Marquette. She kept repeating the name in her head and replaying his voice saying he loved her. Unlike Stefan, who was bold enough to ask her to say it again, she was too nervous to get him to repeat himself. Still, she had heard it the first time.

He loves me. Me!

Stefan's gaze slipped over her body. They had removed their clothes, so she lay naked before him. She realized as he lingered on her breasts that Stefan had seen her as a woman from day one. Hell, she'd have had to be blind not to spot his desire. The way his big cock got so hard and the way he liked to suck her nipples, plucking at them, the man knew what he was getting.

Talicia arched up, offering him her body, and his eyes seemed to blaze hotter. He leaned down and snaked his tongue over one nipple. She tried to suppress a groan, but it slipped out. Her pussy clenched.

"Your nipples are so tight," he murmured.

"They tend to do that when you lick them."

"I haven't started yet."

He pinched a bud between two fingers and pulled gently. Desire shot through her. She squirmed. The stimulation was too much and not enough. She started to cover her other breast to give it some action herself, but Stefan knocked her hand away.

"That belongs to me. Leave it alone."

"You like when I play with myself."

"Not when I'm playing."

The selfish man sucked one nipple into his mouth and pinched the other between his thumb and forefingers. He rolled the tip of one and flicked the other. She drew her knees up and arched closer to him.

"Stefan, you're killing me. Feels so good."

He murmured something against her skin that sounded like, "tastes good too," but she wasn't sure. The pressure increased until the tiniest of aches started in her nipple. He pinched harder, so not like Stefan. She was on the edge of an orgasm with just him messing with her boobs.

Stefan began to lick and suck faster. He plucked her peak at a rate that drove her insane. She pushed at his shoulders then pulled on his arms. "I think I'm going to come, Stefan."

She shouted his name, but before she crashed over the other side, he pushed a hand between her legs to cup her mound. The heel of his palm pressed against her swollen bud. She was losing it fast. Talicia began pumping up to his hand, but he moved it again.

"No, please, Stefan!"

"Honey, I'll never leave you unsatisfied."

He moved down her body and slipped his hands under her hips to grasp her ass cheeks. Raising her hips off the bed, he delved between her legs with his tongue and homed in on her pussy. One slice of his tongue over her folds, and she bit down on a screech. Another, and she shuddered from her head to her feet.

Stefan raised her higher. He sucked hard at her opening and licked the cream that had already wet her entrance from the first moment he began to stimulate her body. His moan sent vibrations through her system.

"So delicious." He delved deeper and burrowed into her heat. She wiggled her hips to get him as far as he could go.

Eat me. She wanted to say it out loud but had never spoken that dirty to Stefan. *Eat my pussy, please, Stefan.*

He stopped and gazed up at her. She balled the sheets in her fists. His lips were moist with her come. What a turn-on to look at this sexy man, crazy over her. She saw the love and lust in his expression, and her heart threatened to burst. That aside, dirty words still trembled on her lips, and she decided to test them out.

"I want to come so bad, Stefan. Please, eat my pussy."

His fingers spasmed on her butt. Was it a positive or a negative? His green eyes darkened to the point that they almost looked black. He lowered his head and started licking her clit, sucking it between his lips, teasing her until she couldn't take it anymore.

"I can't, I can't, I can't," she shouted. Oh, hell, yes, she could. Her orgasm raged over her. She shouted his name loud enough for anyone in the hall or the surrounding rooms to hear. They might have heard it on Mars for all she cared.

Vibrations rumbled through her body, and Stefan kept sucking all the way through it. She grabbed the back of his head and pumped into his mouth, feeding him all he wanted. When she at last collapsed, he eased off and let her catch her breath.

Slowly, he crawled up the bed to arrive where he started, on his knees above her. "Look at me, Licia."

She had shut her eyes, but at his prompting, she focused on him. He ran a thumb over his lips and sucked it clean. Damn man. She loved him so much. He sat up and grabbed her hand to settle on his cock. The thick tool throbbed under her fingers.

"After that I'm about to burst. Sit on my lap."

He helped her to climb up as he sat on his haunches. Talicia wrapped her legs around his waist as she faced him and held onto his shoulders. Stefan started off slow and easy. Then he began to bounce her like he hadn't done before, hard and fast, rough and absolutely amazing. Within a few minutes, he was calling out her name, almost as loud as she had been, grinding into her pussy.

Hot come flooded her channel, and Talicia sagged onto Stefan's shoulder. Even a gentle man had untamed sexual needs. She couldn't be happier with him. They stayed connected with him inside her and her on his lap. Neither moved, and Talicia scarcely drew a breath. No one knocked, and she was just happy to stay in her man's arms as long as possible.

* * * *

"I'm not going, sis," Tyjon said for the fourth time.

"You're not serious, Ty. It's dangerous to stay here, and who's going to take care of you?"

He flushed. "I'm the same age as you, and you've been doing it all my life. Enough is enough. I'm a man, and I can make the decision for myself. I've decided. I'm staying."

Tears filled her eyes, and she grabbed her brother's

hands as they all stood in Creed's living room. "Tyjon, please see reason. Stefan, tell him."

"Ty, you're free to come with us. I don't have a problem supporting you and Licia."

"Well I do," he snapped, but Talicia could see he was nervous. Her brother was trying to be independent at the worst possible time. They had already delayed leaving by hours, waiting until nightfall. Now he was putting up a stink when they were ready to walk out the door.

Tyjon cut his gaze to one of the bodyguards, and she groaned. "Ty, there are plenty of men in the world. You can't make stupid decisions that could lose you your life based on one."

Everyone's heads swiveled from Tyjon to the bodyguard and back again, and Talicia could just feel Tyjon digging his heels in. She'd handled it the wrong way and embarrassed him in front of everyone.

"I'm sorry, Ty."

"It's fine." He raised his chin, his lips pursed and fake lashes fluttering. "I'm going to take care of myself from now on, Licia. You can go or stay, but I've said my piece."

Tyjon pranced out of the room, and Talicia heard his steps on the stairs heading to the second floor. She rolled her eyes and rubbed a hand over her forehead. "He made a big production, but he didn't decide to move out of Creed's house."

Stefan chuckled. "Don't worry. I'll set someone to watch over him, and he can live at my place as long as he wants."

The four Marquette men came together, each shaking Stefan's hand. Creed was the one to speak first. "Are you sure about this?"

Stefan pushed his hand aside and hugged Creed.

"You don't sound like you're trying to change my mind anymore."

"No. I think it's pretty clear how you feel about her."

"That's right." Stefan raised his voice. "I love my wife."

Talicia shook her head. "Okay, the world knows, Stefan."

He winked at her.

Jerome opened the front door and walked in. "We're ready for you guys."

Stefan nodded and said good-bye to his brothers again. Damen strode forward and gave Talicia an awkward hug. "Take care of him for me."

"Sure," she said.

Creed nodded at her but kept his distance. Duke raised her off her feet in a bear hug, and Stefan tried to remove his arm from the socket.

"Enough, Duke," Creed barked.

Heaven strode closer. "I didn't really get to know you, but maybe when you come back and this is all over. We can talk."

"I'd like that," Talicia told her and couldn't help her gaze sliding to Shada. The woman stood beside her husband, rubbing her belly and looking bitter. At last she wandered next to Heaven. To Talicia's shock, she leaned in and hugged her.

"Hurt him, and I break you," she whispered. "But…um…love him, okay?"

Talicia drew back and sniffed, nodding. "I will."

In the car, Talicia held onto Stefan's hand tight enough to crush it. He let her hold him as her stomach rocked and rolled with each bump in the road. She was terrified at any second they would hear a shot and Jerome would shout, "Get down."

Two cars escorted them, one in front and one behind. They had planned out the route to the airport, and so far everything was going smoothly. Once they were on airport grounds, Talicia breathed a little easier. Stefan rubbed her back.

"Okay?" he said.

"I'm fine." She moved to climb out of the car, and on the sidewalk she faced him. He drew her to his side.

"Let the guys handle the luggage. We'll check in."

She moved like a robot. Talicia had never been anywhere outside the United States or for that matter outside Louisiana. She should have been excited about the trip, but she was a ball of nerves. When they approached the long line of people waiting to get through security, she saw the guards and it somehow made her feel better.

Talicia started to get onto the end of the line, but Stefan shook his head and tugged her away. "Not there. We have express service."

"Oh." She found herself in a private lounge after security was a breeze. Stefan set a drink before her, and she downed it in a couple gulps. The alcohol burned a little but started right away to calm her. "Do you have a private jet?"

He chuckled. "No, but I suppose I could have one. I always enjoyed being around other people. First class was good enough. You look disappointed."

"I'm not."

"Shall I buy one just for you?"

"Don't be ridiculous, Stefan." She grinned and kissed him. "Thanks for the offer. I just can't believe we're going to be together from now on. It feels like a dream come true. Every time you left the club and I knew you wouldn't be back for a while, it killed me."

"Never again, honey." He wrapped an arm around her shoulders. "I had stupid reasons for staying away. I didn't want to remind my brothers of that life, the club and you being a club owner."

"That life? Were you performers?"

"No, our dad. I'll tell you about it sometime."

"Bad memories?"

"Yes, but not all bad. It drew Creed and Damen and me closer together."

"You're going to miss them."

"I've flown all over the world, but I've always returned to my brothers. Yes, I'll miss them, especially not knowing how long this trip will last. What I wanted most was to never be tied down, but all of a sudden I miss it. I want that life—with you."

"The restaurant and the guys, all of you working together at Marquette's?"

"Yeah."

"Oh, Stefan." She stroked his face. "Don't be sad. I'm so sorry for bringing this on you."

"I'm not sad. I'm with my beautiful wife, and it's not forever."

Talicia dozed while they waited for the boarding call for their flight. A man's deep voice woke her, and she squinted across the way to see Jerome talking on his phone. She hadn't noticed him before, but of course he would travel with them. Where Stefan went, he went.

She sat up and stretched. Stefan's hand roamed over her back. "Nice sleep?"

"Yeah, are we boarding yet?"

Before he could answer, the announcement came over the intercom. He stood and held out his hand, and she took it to rise.

"Stefan, hold on," Jerome said, urgency in his tone.

Talicia's stomach knotted. Stefan's cell phone rang, and he fished it from his pocket to check the display. She looked too. Damen was calling. "He knows we're about to board," Stefan said, but he answered. "Damen, what's up?"

Talicia pressed closer to him to try to listen. Damen's voice came out too tinny to understand, so she stretched up to the tip of her toes. She heard him this time, and her world tilted.

"Say that again," Stefan urged.

"I said Marquette's is on fire, and Shada just went into labor," Damen explained. "We're on our way to the hospital, but Duke went to the restaurant to check things out about an hour ago. I can't get him on the phone. I've sent a couple guards. We'll keep you updated."

"The hell you will," Stefan growled.

"Calm down. We'll get this straightened out."

Stefan disconnected the call and started dialing again with one hand as he grabbed Talicia's hand with the other. "Honey, stick close to me. Jerome, you get us to Marquette's. If you dare to disobey, I'll fire you."

CHAPTER EIGHTEEN

The greatest fear Talicia ever felt in her life was when they neared St. Louis Street and balls of smoke and fire lit the night sky. Then Stefan told her he intended to go inside to rescue his cousin.

"No," she screamed, and tears streamed down her face. "Jerome, you stop him! Keep driving if you have to."

Jerome had to stop the car because of the traffic jam, the fire trucks and police cars blocking traffic and a crowd of onlookers. Stefan threw his door open and started toward the block where his beloved restaurant lay. Jerome moved in front of him.

"Stefan, don't do this. Get back in the car and let me take you and your wife somewhere safe."

"First the club then Marquette's," Stefan said, his jaw tight.

"I know, but you and her are more important."

"We're fine. What about Duke?"

"He can take care of himself."

"Get out of my way, Jerome!"

They went chest to chest. Stefan was big, but so was

Jerome, and he was trained to take a man down. Talicia stood close to Stefan and scanned the crowd. She felt like they were sitting ducks out there, waiting for someone to pick them off. Sure there were a lot of eyes, but wasn't that how it worked in the movies? So many people, but no one saw it happen?

She tugged his arm. "Stefan, Jerome is right. We should go."

"I know they weren't nice to you, honey, but they're my family too. I can't stand by and wait to see if Duke is hurt."

"What about Shada?" she said.

He frowned at her. "Creed is with her."

She reached up and squeezed his chin. "Stefan, she's five months pregnant. She shouldn't be in labor. They could lose the baby, and she could be in danger too. Don't you think Creed's scared right now?"

He paled. "I hadn't…Oh, no. This isn't happening."

They were back in the car headed toward the hospital. Talicia looked over her shoulder at the water in the distance shooting toward the restaurant as it burned. Other buildings in the block were in danger. She wouldn't believe this was an accident, and it would kill her to think Duke might be hurt or dead because of it.

A short while later, they found Damen, Heaven, and the kids in the waiting room. Stefan strode up to his brother and hugged him. "Where is he?"

"Back with her," Damen said. "I told you not to come."

"You knew that didn't mean anything."

They sat down, and Talicia moved to Heaven's side. "What happened?"

"I don't know." Her face was wet with tears. "She was okay, and we were talking. Then the call came in about the restaurant. I think the shock did it. Shada loves Marquette's as much, maybe more, than the guys. She's just got to be okay, and the baby. For her to have this happen after she was so scared to have kids and a family, it's unfair."

Talicia had thought of the woman as an evil bitch from the day she met her, but her feelings softened. Shada must be terrified and Creed beside himself. She glanced at the two brothers waiting. Both of them looked pale, and they both clutched their phones in their hands as if they waited for news of Duke.

Heaven noticed too. "Damen and Duke argue like they hate each other, but it was killing him to stay here and not go looking for Duke. He sent men over there, but he had to stay with Creed just in case."

Talicia nodded. She held her hand out, and Heaven took it. They clung to each other as time passed at a snail's pace. After some time, Heaven gave in to the strain and began to doze. Her husband walked over to them to take her in his arms. Talicia returned to her husband's side, and he hugged her.

Stefan dropped his face against her chest, and she wrapped her arms as tight as she could around him. A shudder rocked him, and she knew he was scared. He adored his family, and he'd just been talking about how hard it was to be away from them without knowing how long. Then this had to happen. If he resented her after it was all over, she wouldn't be surprised or blame him.

The night was slow going. Talicia had no idea why it took so long, but all she knew was she woke up on Stefan's lap and quickly climbed down, embarrassed. Eyes of curious patients around the room stared at them, but none sat nearby. She supposed it had to do with the monster guards looking so threatening.

Creed walked out from the back, and Damen and Stefan pounced on him. "Well?" Stefan demanded, almost shaking his oldest brother.

Creed looked dead on his feet, and he hadn't yet removed the scrubs the staff had made him wear. "I have a son," he whispered. "He can fit in the palm of my hand, but he's alive."

Creed's voice cracked, and Stefan crushed him in a hug. "What about Shada?"

"She's okay. It was touch and go for a while, but she'll be okay too. The baby has to stay here for now."

"Of course." Damen shook Creed's hand, smiling. "Congratulations, Dad. You're initiated into fatherhood. How's it feel?"

"Exhausting."

"You haven't seen the half of it yet."

No one said anything about Duke, but Creed noticed. "Where is he?"

"Just concentrate on your wife and son," Damen said. "Duke is fine."

Creed frowned and looked at Stefan. "Where is Duke, Stefan?"

"We're looking for him. I'm sure he's okay, Creed. Damen is right. You need to concentrate on your family."

Creed spun away from his brothers. "Pete," he barked, and half the waiting room jumped a foot in the air, including Talicia. The guard was at his elbow in a heartbeat. "You find my cousin. You make sure he's okay, and you let me know. Do it now."

"Yes, sir, Mr. Creed."

Creed returned to Shada and their son, and when Talicia started to sway and Heaven didn't appear any better condition, the family left the hospital. The next morning, Talicia woke in bed alone. She dressed quickly and hurried to the first floor. The men were talking in the kitchen with Heaven at the table.

Talicia accepted a cup of coffee from Stefan and took a sip. "Duke?"

"Nothing," he said. "But there's also no evidence that he was caught in the blaze."

Talicia pressed a hand to her chest and sighed in relief. "That's good. Was the fire department able to save it?"

Damen cursed, and his wife pulled him into her arms. He gave in to her for a minute and then put her from him to pace. "No. Our restaurant has been destroyed."

"I—" Talicia began.

He shook his head. "Don't. We don't blame you, Talicia. You're family now. What I am worried about is my cousin. We have our differences, and he's an asshole, but damn it, he better be okay."

"You're breaking my heart, cuz. I didn't know you loved me so much."

They all whipped around to face the kitchen doorway. There stood a dirty and obviously worn out Duke. Stefan reached him first and dragged him into a chair. "What happened to you, Duke?"

Talicia looked from Duke to Damen and watched as her brother-in-law stared daggers at Duke while seeming relieved at the same time. He remained leaning against the kitchen counter as if he didn't trust himself to approach Duke.

"It's a long story," Duke said, full of himself, "and I'll tell you all about it. The gist is that I followed someone away from the restaurant."

"Who?" Damen demanded.

Duke flexed his fingers and pressed a knuckle to his lips. That's when Talicia noticed how busted up they were. His skin was bruised and torn in spots. Duke met her concerned gaze and grinned. "You don't have to worry anymore, little cousin. I got him."

"Got *who?*" Stefan emphasized.

"Marcus Colby."

"Y-you killed him?" Talicia asked and swallowed.

"It's not the first time, and it probably won't be the last." Duke removed the shaking coffee cup from her fingers and drained the contents. "You're safe, and yeah, we're going to have to rebuild the restaurant, but we're all alive, got it? All of the Marquettes are alive."

Damen moved across the kitchen to stand behind Duke's chair. He leaned down and kissed the top of his head, slapping heavy hands on his cousin's shoulders.

Stefan met Talicia's gaze. "Yeah, we'll rebuild, all of us together, as a family."

She sniffed and nodded, sure that he was right.

The End

CPSIA information can be obtained at www.ICGtesting.com
Printed in the USA
LVOW06s1125171215

466988LV00001B/48/P